PRECIOUS NORMAN

HONOR

BY A.L. STUMO

Published April 2011
Kathmirrid Press
1116 West Second Street
Pella, Iowa 50219 USA
ISBN 978-0983484707

Cover Illustration by Richard Sanchez

BRIDGNORTH CASTLE IN SHROPSHIRE, ENGLAND IN MAY OF THE YEAR 1102

DAY 1, THURSDAY

"They must be here. Hurry up, Maud." Rowena yelled as she finished coiling her fishing line.

I was pulling in my fishing line and coiling it as fast as I could. Rowena was beside me, leaning over the riverbank, pulling our net of fish out of the water. The horn sounded a second time. I came to the hook at the end of the line and turned; she was already bounding up the steep hill like a doe. I chased after her while holding the hem of my dress and the coiled line, but I knew I could never catch her. I had to work harder to avoid tripping over tree roots. I thought, *How can she see the roots fast enough to move like that? Will I be able to move so fast when I am thirteen? No, probably not. She has always been quicker and more graceful.*

Someone blew the horn again, third time. I needed to hurry. My father had told us to be back before the horn sounded a fourth time.

The wooden roof of the new church came into

view ahead. The top of the hill was close. I could no longer see Rowena ahead. I thought, *Is she already inside the castle walls?* I ran between the wooden wall of the church and the new limestone wall of the castle.

Mother was standing inside the open, wooden gates. As I ran to her, I heard the horn again. She gave me a reassuring hug and then released me.

"Put the smelly fishing gear away," she said. "Wait for me by the kitchen. I have to wait here to help the priest carry his things." Her brown braids swinging slightly, she turned her head away to look at the church door. I inched around her so I could look in her brown eyes.

"Why is *he* bringing his things in here?" I asked.

She gave me her impatient look. "He will have to stay inside the castle walls with the rest of us for safety. Now, go put that fishing gear away."

I looked out the gates and down the hill. "Are they here yet? I can not see anyone marching up the road." All I could see was the dirt road and trees on the hill leading to St. Leonard's church.

"Do you want help carrying the priest's things?"

Mother put her hand under my chin and spoke very deliberately. "No, my dear child, go put that gear away."

I knew better than to let her voice go from deliberate to angry. I ran to the west wall of the stable where the fishing gear hung on pegs. Rowena had already hung hers up and disappeared. The stable and the smithy beside it were deserted. Two of the horses were gone.

I jogged back to the yard in front of the kitchen. Two Saxon man-servants and the priest came running back through the gates with their arms full of altar linens, chalice, plate, candles, and candlesticks. The servants must have run to help at the first horn. That explained why no one was back in the horse stable.

Coming towards the gates again, I spied two of the Norman men-at-arms bringing two horses in through the gates. Father, with his left hand on the sword at his belt, jogged over to them and pointed towards the stable. I ran to his side. He was telling the men to take the doe back to the cobblestones where they could gut the deer.

"Father," I asked, "may I go back out to see where the army is? Or do you have an errand for me out there? Do you need anything from down by the river?"

"No," he said, "we must stay in here now."

Father smiled at me and motioned for me to stay where I was. He walked briskly to the castle gates. He leaned his slender body against the eastern gate to help Sir Jehann, the chief man-at-arms, close the rough-hewn wooden gate, which was three times the height of a man.

Moving the heavy gate only a few inches, Father yelled, "Come here and help! Now!"

As was the way with his commands, four men and I ran to shove the gates shut. We worked together, with me wedged between Saxon servants with woolly beards and hair in a braid and Norman men-at-arms with short hair and clean-shaved faces.

I thought, *Surely, these heavy gates will keep King Henry and his army out. What could be sturdier?*

Once the gates were shut he yelled, "Everyone go back to what you were doing. The army will take two hours at least to march to the castle." Because my father was the castle seneschal, he was in charge of when to open or shut the gates.

Why, I thought, *do the gates have to be shut right now? Two hours is plenty of time to run more errands.*

I opened my mouth to ask this aloud, but Father put a finger to his lips to signal quiet and then pointed to the kitchen. I started walking slowly towards the smell of fish guts. Rowena was in there cleaning our fish.

The shutters on the windows of the thatch-roofed kitchen were wide open. Mildred, the head cook, must have been predicting a sunny day. I poked my head through the doorway and saw my friend Rowena at my

4

mother's work table by the door.

Rowena saw me too. "Get over here, Maud."

"Why are you bossing me?" I came over to the table anyway.

"Sorry," she said sincerely. "I will clean my three fish, but I am not cleaning your one."

I thought, *Why does she have to remind me that I did not catch as many as her?*

Rowena looked upset, as if she was holding back tears. She was finishing taking the scales off the third fish.

"Is that my fish over there?" I asked.

She nodded and I grabbed a fish knife at the back of the table. The table was more than long enough for us to stand side by side.

"Why did you come do this and miss all the excitement outside?"

She stared at the fish. "You want to see the gates close? You want to see our imprisonment here start?"

I was about to reply no, when women came in through the kitchen door and distracted me. Mother and Mildred, the chief cook, were discussing what to serve for midday meal. The other two cooks were walking behind them, listening.

Rowena was now cutting her fish into chunks for frying. I was still working on removing the scales on mine.

Mother came over to inspect how many fish we had caught. Then she spoke to Mildred over by the fireplace. "Looks like enough for everyone to have a taste, but not enough for a full portion."

Mildred looked into a pot hanging over the fireplace. "Mmm. That and stew and bread should do. We need to start being frugal."

I whispered to Rowena, "Can you feel all the excitement?"

"Can you feel all the dread?" she whispered back. "I am going to clean my knife. You clean your knife and the table, right?"

I knew the table was clean when I could no longer smell the fish in the wood. I joined Rowena at the kitchen doorway. She pointed at me and then at herself and then at the tower. I thought, *She wants to climb up on the watch tower.*

I nodded, and she started walking confidently to the northwest corner of the castle, towards the entrance of the watch tower. I looked around. The men were all running about. I thought, *Good, none of them will notice us.*

I caught up with her at the entrance of the newly-built wooden tower. We both walked to the thirty-foot tall ladder inside. I thought, *Will the dark in here keep the men from seeing us climb up?* I could see the hem of Father's blue tunic. He was standing beside the top of the ladder. *Aargh. Surprise is no longer an option.*

Rowena nudged me in the ribs.

"Father," I called up. "May we come up there?"

He looked down the ladder. His brown eyes were scanning in the dim light.

"It is you two. No." Then he hesitated. "Why?"

I gathered my best hopeful voice. "We wish to see the King's army. You said they are still miles away. Please?"

He scowled. "No place here for curious children. Go away." He straightened and disappeared from view.

"What do we do now?" I asked.

She shrugged. "Maybe he will let us up there later. We should not have been so fast running up the hillside. We could have seen something from outside, behind the church, maybe."

"We would have been in so much trouble with our parents if we had dawdled," I said. I moved away from the ladder, thinking, *Father will probably yell soon if he does not see me walking away from the tower. What will happen if I cannot see out? How will I know what is happening?*

Rowena grabbed my hand and made me slow

down. "I think it better to be a wild animal out there avoiding hunters than a penned animal in here waiting for the butcher."

"We are not animals," I said. "We will be fine. Father says the siege will only last a few days. No one in here will die. Look at those thick walls. What could get through those?"

She stopped and stared at me. "You are so innocent."

I returned her gaze. "You always think the worst."

We were back at the kitchen door. She stuck her tongue out at me and wandered a few paces off.

I looked over at the gates and then shut my eyes. In my mind, the gates were open. Earl Robert of Belesme, a burly man in armor, was riding his huge brown stallion up the northern road towards Bridgnorth Castle, his castle. He had eight knights behind him on their war horses. The Earl was dressed the same as when he had ridden out of here only eight days ago. Behind the knights, the Earl had a long column of Welsh soldiers, walking four abreast. The Welshmen trailed down the dirt road. Our army of rescuers will be an immense army, so I tried to fill the army with Welsh faces I had seen this winter.

Rowena broke in on my thoughts. "I see my little brother, Edric, over at the pigsty. The piglets are still in the cute stage. Come on."

I followed her.

***

"Urgh! I cannot get these stitches right," I complained.

"Calm down," replied my cousin Aethel.

About an hour after midday dinner, Aethel and I were practicing knitting. We were sitting on the ground outside the kitchen. Aethel's grandmother, Mildred, had started teaching us knitting in December on Aethel's tenth birthday. We were now able to make badly shaped socks out of the wool yarn scraps that were in balls at our feet.

Aethel's pudgy fingers were gripping yellow yarn very loosely. She was knitting a sock she had intended for herself, but which was turning out to be big enough for her seventeen year-old brother.

My un-dyed yarn had started as a sock big enough for Mother, but as I knitted closer to the ankle the stocking was becoming small enough for a little child. Each new row was smaller, though the number of stitches was the same. Mildred had told me to make the stitches bigger, but telling me was not making it happen.

"Where were you," I asked Aethel, "when the horn sounded? I did not see you when I came in."

Aethel stopped knitting. "I was sent out at the last second. When great-uncle Wulfstan sounded the horn for the first time Grandmother handed the kitchen mama cat to me and told me to take her as far outside as I could before the fourth horn. So I ran north to the yew stumps and dropped her and ran back here. Well, I did not really have to drop her. She was so mad at being carried that she jumped out of my arms and took off. When I saw those Normans bringing the horses in I was afraid I might be locked out, but I made it back in time."

"Oh," I answered. "I did not see you."

"Mmm, I went back to the stables with the mare once they lifted the doe off her. I had to get her unsaddled and brushed."

"I wish I could have been the one to do that," I said. I like grooming Father's mare.

She shrugged and went back to knitting. I rubbed my hands on the ball of wool. The lanolin made my hands feel soft.

We were both knitting, when one of men standing watch on the tower yelled, "Look! The army!"

We stood up as all the men in the castle ran over to the entrance of the wooden watch tower. The tower had been built right up against the stone wall near the gate. The tower timbers were anchored into the massive, thirty foot high wall. I wondered if the limestone wall looked as impressive to the King's army as it did to me.

I thought, *Should I try to get up there to see now?* Father and two Saxon men standing watch were facing south, back over the castle grounds and beyond the castle. *They must be seeing the army in the valley to the south of us.*

I walked over to the corner of the kitchen so that I could see the south wall too. The castle walls had been built on this steep hill above the River Severn this fall and winter to fortify the wooden Saxon fort that had been here for more than a century. My father had told me that Earl Robert believed the excellent view this hill provided was well worth defending with five foot thick stone walls. From this castle, one could see to the south to protect the Norman-owned and Saxon-run farms and to the west to spy on the sometimes enemy, sometimes ally Welsh.

I caught myself fidgeting, playing with my wooden cross necklace. I heard people moving around the castle yard behind me. I looked around. Little Edric was in tears, as he clung on to Rowena's tunic. Rowena displayed her being-brave face. Mother's lips were drawn tight, as if she were doing something unpleasant. Sir Jehann had the same expression on his face. I noticed he now wore his coat of chain mail over his blue tunic.

I walked over to stand by Mother. She nodded to me and took my hand.

"Why did the Earl not stay here behind the castle walls with the rest of us?" I asked her. "We would be far safer with the Earl and his knights here."

"Maud," she said in her patience-being-strained voice. "Earl Robert has this castle, two other castles and all the lands around them to protect from the army of King Henry. He has to take care of many places. Now, hush."

Sir Jehann went into the tower and started to climb the ladder, but Father reminded him that the tower was only meant to hold three men. So Jehann stopped and climbed back down slowly. By the look on his face, he would be sure to stand guard next.

The three men up on the platform did not move or speak. All of us down below were standing and waiting. I thought, *What are we waiting for? I can hear nothing outside.*

As the excitement seemed over for the moment, Aethel and I went back to knitting outside the kitchen, but it was hard to concentrate.

It became even harder to concentrate an hour later when we could hear the faint sound of horses, wagons and marching feet from the King's army. The noise continued for a long time until it sounded like the many horses and wagons of the army were at the bottom of the steep hill.

Father, William and Sir Jehann were on the watch tower. Sir Jehann had replaced Wulfstan as I had expected, and William, a Norman man-at-arms, had replaced Bert.

I heard horns blowing from outside. Rowena came over and waved to us. All three of us moved over through the garden to the western wall near the tower. We could faintly hear someone shouting in French.

Then Sir Jehann uscd his stout lungs to shout in French back at them. I could make out some of what he was saying. My father had taught me some of his native language. Jehann was saying, "King Henry has no place here…Earl Robert is our man…these thick walls…he shall return…with a large army…go."

The angry man's voice started shouting again. He shouted a long time. He must be up on the hilltop on the other side of the wall, I realized, for his voice to carry so well.

This time Father shouted back, "No." *Well, no is clear enough to understand*, I thought, *even in French*. Aethel leaned towards me and asked quietly what the King's men were saying. I shook my head and whispered that I could not make it out.

I could hear the hooves of the horses start cantering back down the hill.

My father looked over the railing of the tower and spotted us down below. He smiled when he saw me.

"Go tell your mother that the army will camp tonight and come back to shout at us again tomorrow. She is to get supper ready. No fighting tonight."

I ran back to the kitchen to deliver the message. I thought, *Perhaps if I run my errand well, Father will let me look later.*

***

One of my chores is to help carry all meals from the kitchen to the great hall. That night, I glanced around the castle yard from the kitchen doorway. I could not see any signs of attack, though I was not sure what the signs of attack would be.

As I entered the hall, the round stone fireplace in the center of the hall was giving the whole building light and heat. I was in the main room that ran the length of the hall and was where all of us servants and men-at-arms slept and ate. Ahead were the heavy, woven wall hangings along the back wall. Behind the hangings were three rooms. Off to my left, was the men's dressing room where I never went. Off to my right was the women's dressing room where I went twice a day. In front of me was the Earl's bedroom where I was never to go.

I wondered, *What is it like to have a bed chamber all to oneself. Is it too lonely? No, if it is lonely, a man as powerful as the Earl would order us to keep him company.*

That night in the great hall, five tables were set up for supper. The head table was between the fireplace and the center wall hanging. Four other tables were on the other side of the fireplace facing the head table.

Rowena and I carried pitchers of weak ale for the head table and adult tables. Aethel carried the water pitcher for the children's table where we always sat.

I started shivering from cold in the chilly, evening air. I heard a few adults at the servants' table grumble about not being able to have an evening fire and how a fire was still necessary in early May. Despite being cold, I stayed where I was and did not fetch myself a cloak from the dressing room.

When most people had finished eating, Father stood up to speak. He was up at the head table where he sat with my mother and Sir Jehann. Standing in his blue tunic, everyone looked up from their plates and mugs.

"As you all heard this afternoon," he began, "King Henry's army has arrived. The King is not here. The army is led by Lord Roger de Montgomery. Sir Jehann and I have spoken to Lord Roger. He intends to take this castle. Whether he will attack or lay a siege, we do not yet know."

"What we do know is that our sworn liege, Earl Robert of Belesme, told us to hold this castle. We do not surrender. He is even now in Shrewsbury where he is concluding his talks with the Welsh princes who supplied two hundred stone masons and laborers to build the castle walls this last year. The Earl has made plans with the Welsh princes to give him an army so that he can fight the army of King Henry of England. He will return from Shrewsbury with this large army of his own. The Earl will send the King's knights running back to their mothers."

My father paused while many of the Saxons laughed at the image of full-grown Norman knights running like babies.

"Yes," he resumed, "you are used to fighting Welsh rebels and hunting their cowardly leaders. Yes, you are not used to siege warfare. But rest assured that Sir Jehann, William, Chrestian and I have learned our Norman tactics of sieges and battles well. Bridgnorth will hold until the Earl returns. As the Earl told you before he left, he should be back here within two weeks."

As Father sat back down at the head table, Jehann leaned over to compliment him on the fine speech. Or at least that looked like what he was saying. I could not tell for sure from the other side of the hall.

Rowena leaned over Edric to me and whispered, "By our lady, am I glad that was your father speaking. Jehann might have jabbered all night in that thick accent of his."

I nodded quickly in agreement.

I thought, *Will the army keep Earl Robert away? Are we really in danger of dying?* Images of my mother and father lying dead in the hall filled my mind. I shuddered. I could feel my heart start to beat faster.

I started to eat again to chase away the scary thoughts. It only worked for a minute. Then I was back to wondering what the army looked like and how many knights were there. I realized my mind would not be at ease until I saw them.

When I finished eating, I helped to clear the mugs off the tables. Clearing them after meals was another one of my chores. Some mugs I could carry two in a hand and others four in a hand. No one potter had made them, so they were in no one size. The sun had recently set, so I could not scan the castle yard for signs of attack. I simply walked as fast as I could to the kitchen and hoped.

As soon as the tables were cleared off, the men lifted the tables to the side of the hall at Father's command.

Rowena came up behind me and whispered, "I

will not be able to sleep. I am far too fearful."

What should I say? I feel fear too, but Father will not want me making her worse, I thought.

"It will be fine. The Earl will be back soon," I said, hoping my voice shared my father's confidence.

DAY 2, FRIDAY

I woke some time after dawn and found I was almost alone. Only Rowena was still in the hall, which was not surprising because Rowena was usually the last one up in the morning.

I said good morning, and Rowena grunted in a sleepy way. Once Rowena was standing, we helped each other stack our mattresses on the pile of them at the end of the hall. The task was harder because late-risers had to hoist theirs up on the tall pile that had already been stowed away.

While we were in the dressing room putting on our tunics over the woolen under-dresses that we slept in, we heard rain start hitting the thatch roof. As soon as the rain became a downpour, the door to the hall opened and shut quickly.

When Rowena and I came out of the dressing room, Aethel's older brother Bert, the pig boy, and Rowena's uncle Manfred, the stable groom, were lifting the head table into place for breakfast. Manfred called to us to help.

Rowena grabbed the one oak bench for the head table and put it in place behind the heavy, oak table. As Manfred and Bert moved a table, Rowena and I carried the benches. Each rectangular table had two short benches to go down one long side of the table so that everyone sitting at the table faced the head table. I thought, *How had someone long ago realized that if the benches were exactly this long then each bench could fit under the table between meals?*

Bert and Manfred finished first and stood off to the side to keep out of our way.

"Rowena," said Manfred in the voice he used for teasing, "are you ready to get working?"

"Very funny, uncle," she replied. "This *is* working."

"Not compared to what you will be doing the rest of the day," he said as he flopped down on one of the benches.

"Oh, and what is that?" she asked playfully.

"You will be doing all the men's chores. We will be defending the castle."

I interrupted, "Has the fighting begun? I did not hear anything." I hoisted one of the benches for the men-at-arms table.

Manfred laughed, a deep hearty laugh, his beard bobbing up and down. He usually found the ignorance of others funny.

Bert was not smiling as he answered me, "No, the

army is having a leisurely breakfast in their camp on the hill to our west."

I tried to imagine a camp over on the sheep pasture hill. The ground was quite uneven, but the top was kept nicely grassed for pasture, which meant the tents were not among trees. The sheep pasture hill's slope rose as quickly as the castle hill dropped down, a slope too steep to carry a pitcher of water without dripping. I burst out, "When can we see the camp?"

Now they were both laughing at me. *That must mean not now*, I thought.

***

At mid-morning, we all heard heavily-laden horses climbing the path up the hill that lead to the gate. Everyone approached the tower and gates as close as they could. I heard the horses stop and then I heard a shout from beyond the wall. Unfortunately, I could not get close to the wall like I had the day before. The men who were not up in the tower were over by the gates trying to hear. Well, except for Father Cuthbert, the priest, and Rowena's father Godwin, the blacksmith, who were over at the east wall of the castle stacking stones to create a make-shift altar.

I heard the sound of shouting from outside. It went

on for several minutes. I tugged at blades of grass with my toes. Like the day before, I could not make out what the voice was saying. Perhaps the speaker was from some other part of France and not from Normandy. My father had once told me that Normans spoke a French different from the others.

Sir Jehann responded in French. The only words that I could understand were no, please, Earl Robert, castle, water and meat. I was surprised; usually I can understand most of what he says.

The shouting resumed from outside. It went on forever and made my stomach feel tight. I had the same kind of feeling when I watched my parents argue: wishing to stop it, wishing to walk away, wishing to watch, and wishing to yell back.

When the shouting ended, I could see the helmet on Father's head and the shoulders and helmet of Sir Jehann on the tower platform. I could hear them talking together angrily. I thought, *Oh, if only I could hear what they are saying. If only I could have understand what the knight outside said.*

Jehann leaned over the tower railing nearest the gate and shouted "No." One word in reply, after all that.

I heard some laughter from King Henry's knights and heard the clopping of hooves as their horses moved back down the hill. Jehann picked up a stone and threw it over the wall.

I thought, *Is he trying to hit those knights? Is the talking over? Will we go back to chores?* I looked around at the others, no one was moving. All were staring at the tower. *What are they waiting for? Will Father make another speech? Will Father open the gates so the men can go fight?*

Father did not make another speech. He came down the ladder, and William, a Norman man-at-arms, climbed up with a large canvas sack of small rocks over his shoulder. Placing my hand over my eyes, I stepped back to see better what they were doing on the watch tower. William climbed to the top to join his younger brother Chrestian and Sir Jehann. They loaded rocks, the size of my fist, into the sling poles that each one held. Each sling pole was a five foot tall wooden pole, with a hole near the top through which several small ropes were tied. In the loop of each rope was a piece of leather that acted as a pouch for the rock until it was thrown. I could see William loading a rock in the pouch. He lowered the pole back until the rock was hanging loose and then quickly raised the pole. The rock sprang out of the leather and shot over the wall.

I ran over to Father in the base of the tower,

tugged on his left sleeve and asked him, "What is William doing? Will that not make the knights angry?"

He looked into my face and chuckled. "They are angry already, my dear one. Soon they will throw rocks at us, so we will get a few shots in while we can."

Then he stopped talking and looked at me as if he had not seen me there before. "Get all the women and children indoors," he said to Mother. "Soon it will be unsafe here in the castle yard."

How large will the stones be that the King's knights will throw? I wondered.

I did not get to see stones coming over the wall. Aethel, Rowena and I spent the rest of the day in the kitchen. From there, we could hear sharp noises of stones hitting the stone wall, but no thuds of stones hitting the ground out in the castle yard.

We knitted socks. As we sat there, I paused and looked over at Rowena. "Should we try to sneak up on the tower tonight? We could say we were going to the privies and then go there instead."

Rowena looked at me condescendingly. "If it is dark enough to make us unseen then the army camp will be dark and impossible to see, right?"

"Oh, yes."

"We must find a way to get up there in daylight."

I nodded. Somehow we must find an excuse. I thought about it, but could see no excuse that would not be either laughed at or ignored.

"I am bored of knitting," said Rowena.

"What do you want to do next?" I gladly put my knitting back in the basket beside me.

"Go outside and see what is going on." Rowena was also putting her knitting away.

"We cannot do that," replied Aethel.

"I know that," Rowena said with a sarcastic snarl. "But we can not simply sit here in this prison doing nothing, seeing nothing."

"We could get sticks and play tic-tac-toe right here," I suggested.

Aethel nodded.

Mildred standing at her work table near us, scowled down. "You will not scratch this firm floor with those sticks. Takes a lot of work to get it this way."

"Yes, ma'am," Aethel and I replied at exactly the same time. We then looked at each other and laughed.

Rowena set her yarn down. "You remember the day last month when we went down to the farm, right? The old farm a mile south of here and watched sheep's fleeces being loaded on a wagon. Remember how that wagon had fleeces piled higher than a tall man could keep upright?"

Aethel and I both nodded and Rowena kept telling the story of how we had helped carry fleeces to the wagon and then watched it leave on the road to Oldbury. She talked until finally Mildred told us supper was finished and ready to be carried to the great hall.

***

I helped carry the pitchers from the kitchen to the great hall. I kept my eyes on the path in front of me to make sure I did not trip as I walked faster than normal from the kitchen. I kept my ears open for any shouts telling us that stones were coming our way. Aethel, in front of me, was carrying five round loaves of wheat bread in a basket. Ulrica, in front of Aethel, was carrying clay bowls full of roast carrots. Mildred and Rowena, were behind me, carrying platters of roast venison. Mildred claimed she had been learning to roast venison for all of her fifty-three years, but I figured to roast something this well and make it smell this delicious had to be a God-given talent and not just practice.

Mildred had carved the venison in the kitchen, slicing it thinly before putting it on the platters. "This way," she had told us on our way out of the kitchen, "we all know how much of it to take."

I thought, *We are being served portions to keep us*

all from eating more than our share.

I set the pitcher down beside Mother at the head table and delivered the other pitchers, one per table. Then I walked back to the end table where all the children sat, including me. I sat down between Aethel and Edric. Edric, being only five, I generally had to pour his water from the heavy pitcher and help him dish foods on his plate. If Rowena got to the table first, she helped him. But usually she was busier with carrying food in than I was. Rowena sat on the other side of Edric now, but next summer when she turned fourteen and became a woman, she would move up the tables to where her father and older sister sat.

Sure enough, as soon as I sat down, Edric's halo of fuzzy brown hair leaned towards me. He opened his mouth to start yelling for food. I clamped my left hand on his shoulder, startling him.

"Edric," I said, "the food will get here when it gets here. Do not make a scene about it. Have some water."

"But I am really hungry," he whined.

I handed him his orange-glazed mug, full of water from the pitcher. "You are always hungry. And you know your place. Because we sit at the last table we are last to eat. Drink this."

I poured myself some water and looked around at the hall while I waited for the food to be handed down.

Handing plates and baskets always takes forever. The hall was hard to see with only a couple of candles on each table. What the candles let me see was the oak table in front of me. It was made of two thin planks that were joined down the center in a pretty curve. The table was a patchwork of stains that had gone through the varnish and down into the grain of the oak. I thought of all the Saxon children who had sat here at this very table in the hundred and fifty years since this hall had been built. If the table was spilled on at least once a day in all that time, then were the stains from the first spill, second spill, or one hundredth spill?

The meal was quiet. I wondered, *Is Rowena right? Perhaps we are all to feel dread, not excitement because of the army outside.*

DAY 3, SATURDAY

At the end of breakfast, Father stood up at the head table and asked everyone to listen. He looked around the room and I wondered what he saw. Four tables of people were watching him intently.

He began to speak, "As we all meet here at meals it works well for me to use this time to tell you what you all should hear equally."

I realized that only two men were missing, Aethel's great-uncle, Wulfstan, and her older brother, Bert. *They must be on watch*, I thought.

"We need to follow some rules until the Earl and his army arrive."

He held up his hands and ticked off a list on his fingers. "No fires in the great hall. Make as few fires in the kitchen as possible. We cut extra wood this spring, but we have no way to go out and gather more. We will have enough if we are careful."

He counted another finger. "No overfeeding of the animals. Give them only what they need to survive. The oats for the horses will be kept in the cellar and must be fetched every day. This will keep from giving them double feed."

He counted a third finger. "No bathing or washing

of clothes. We can not go down to the river for bathing as we did before and we can not waste the rain water collected in the cistern and rain barrels."

He counted a fourth finger. "When rocks or arrows arrive from over the wall, pick them up and stack them in the base of the tower. We collected many rocks over the winter, but we must also use the extras the army is so *kind* to bestow on us."

He counted his thumb. "If the horn sounds once, all should come to the castle yard. If the horn sounds twice, all men are to go to the tower and all women and children are to go to the kitchen."

My father nodded at everyone and walked out of the hall. There would be neither discussion nor questions answered.

My questions were as numerous as the fish in the Severn River. *When exactly will the Earl arrive? Will the Norman men use water to shave or will they grow their beards out like the Saxon men? Will I wash my hands and face before meals? Will I be allowed to take carrots and apples to Father's horses for treats? How can we see in the great hall at night without a log fire? And are these rules necessary for us to survive or are they only rules to make the siege easier?*

I sighed as I realized these questions would swim

downstream and not be answered.

I leaned over to Rowena who was done eating. I asked her, "What shall we do today?"

Rowena glanced around. "We could play a game. Or we could try to get up on the tower?"

I imagined myself climbing the wooden ladder up to the platform on the tower. I hoisted my skirt up to make room for my leg as I clambered onto the wooden planks, standing at the edge of the platform and looking out over the castle yard. How different and small the buildings and animals looked from up there. Then I faced towards the wall and looked west at the army encampment. I saw horses penned up together and canvas tents and -

"Maud," Rowena interrupted. "What do you want to do?"

My answer and enthusiasm were stopped by Mother's callused fingers on my shoulder. "You three," she said, "need to go weed the vegetable garden this morning. If you hear the horn, run inside. Understand?"

We nodded obediently, and she left. Then I grinned at Rowena. She grinned back. We would climb that ladder.

***

I knelt in the vegetable garden picking small

weeds carefully from between the cabbages peeking tender leaves out of the ground. Rowena and Aethel were in the next two rows, beside the massive limestone wall, carefully pulling short leafy weeds from the brown soil. We must be careful to get every weed and careful to get them in one piece, root and all. This sunny May morning, I called out to no one in particular, "Arrgh, telling the weeds from the cabbages is so hard when they are this small."

Rowena was leaning over to weed the row of beans. Her long blonde hair covered her face from my view. She replied without looking up, "The beans are no better."

Aethel was crouching in the row of turnips. She might not have heard me; she did not respond at all. She was weeding busily. This morning I was in the mood to pull slowly and watch the soil give way.

"I am done over here and will be going in now," said Aethel.

"I think I am actually going to beat you this morning, Maud. Why are you going so slowly? We need to try to get on the tower, right?" said Rowena.

I shrugged. I wanted to go up there. But if Mother had us doing chores, we would not get a chance soon.

Rowena stood up and grabbed her basket of weeds.

When I entered the kitchen with my basket of weeds, I set the weeds on Mildred's work table where Mother and she were classifying each weed. They looked an unlikely pair: Mother almost as tall as a man, Mildred shorter than me.

Mildred explained how the weeds would be used. "Girls, all the weeds we can eat will go into today's dinner; all the others will be sent to the stables for the horses. When I get done with sorting them in the baskets, you three girls go take them to Manfred in the stables. I sort and you carry, three times a week - until - all this unpleasantness is over."

We took them back to Manfred and then walked back to the garden. "We can see the tower from here," I said. "So we can plan our climb."

"I am not going up there," said Aethel. "It will be too dangerous. What if a stone comes at us?"

Rowena scowled at her. "Then you stay here, baby. I am going. You too, Maud, right?"

I nodded with a firm jaw.

We told Aethel to go back in the kitchen and stay out of our way. Then Rowena and I walked very leisurely over to the tower. No one was in the base. I nodded to her. As I gripped the ladder, we heard yelling from up on the watch platform, and we stepped back out to the yard to see what was happening up there.

William, in his padded, leather armor, was yelling over the wall in French. I heard him yell, "You come back here," and "I will show." The rest of it was words I did not know, most likely swear words, because Father never taught them to me when he or the other Normans said them.

Rowena looked at me and asked what he was saying.

I stopped listening to William so I could answer. "I can only make out a few words. He seems to be taunting someone."

"Oh," Rowena said in a small voice. "I wish he would not do that."

"Why? Are you afraid?"

Before she could answer, both of us had to move. Rowena's aunt Ulrica was coming up behind us and shooing us towards the kitchen. She was not much taller than me, but her arms were far stronger, so I did not wait for her to get close enough to start shoving.

"Of course," Rowena now answered me. "I am afraid. That army brought swords with them on purpose to kill all of us Saxons and claim the castle." She started walking at a snail's pace, barely enough movement to keep her aunt from shoving.

"How do you know they have swords? Have you seen the army?" As I said this, I realized how ridiculous it must sound.

"Oh, you know they have swords. They are the King's knights."

I am glad, I thought, *she did not laugh at me for that question.*

"Yes," I said. "Do you really think they want to kill us? I think they might be trying to scare us into forsaking the Earl and opening the gates for them."

Rowena stopped and put her hands on her hips. "No, I think they want to kill us, the Saxons. You, little Miss Norman, will be perfectly fine."

Our eyes were drawn to the west wall where a stone had come over the top and landed with a small thud. The rock had fallen so fast. My heart thudded too as I wondered how I would ever be able to duck fast enough. Ulrica looked worried and her meaty hands shoved us the last couple of feet to the kitchen doorway. We stopped in the doorway.

"My mother is a Saxon," I whispered to Rowena.

"Your father," responded Rowena in a nasty tone, "being a Norman makes you a Norman and you know that. You even have a Norman name, Maud."

I paused. I had to cool down before this became a

shouting match. Fighting with Rowena was like trying to swim upstream, you could do it but it generally was not worth the work.

I sighed to let the anger cool and then said, "I am afraid too. But Father says the Earl will be here soon and then the army will go away."

"Go away? Leaving quick as a snap, right?" Rowena snapped her fingers.

"Well, no. Father says there will be a fight."

Now Rowena looked triumphant. "And people are going to get hurt. My father says it will be the Saxons and Welsh who get the most hurt."

I looked at the tower again. I thought, *Rowena can be so hard to persuade some times. Why does she not believe what my father said? He is right.*

The men on the tower were still flinging rocks from sling poles, and Ulrica told us to move further into the kitchen.

***

I spent the afternoon in the kitchen. Rowena, Aethel and I tried to stay out of the way, but it was hard in the crowded room. The kitchen was slightly larger than its contents: the oven, four work tables, the dry sink, the cooking fire, and two cabinets. A cool breeze was coming in the two open windows on the south wall.

"Edric is lucky," I said to no one in particular, "he is allowed to stay out in the smithy with his father. But I have to stay here in the kitchen under the scullery table. Even Rowena is luckier, standing and helping her sister chop vegetables."

At that, Rowena who had heard me looked down and gave me a scowl. "Being made to work is not lucky," she said.

Ulrica who had finished mixing bread dough sat right by Aethel and put her left arm over Aethel's shoulders.

"Is this not a big change from how things were this winter?" she said.

Aethel squirmed under the heavy arm and answered, "Yes. We cannot go outside."

"I do not mean exactly that. I mean that we do not have all those stone cutters, stone lifters, wagon drivers and others to feed all day. While all those men were working on the walls, I had to make 3 dozen loaves of bread each and every day. And now I made dough for only five loaves. And my mother-in-law, who is Rowena's grandmother you know, has gone back to her farm along with Mildred's two daughters, your aunts, who came to help us cook all that food each day," said Ulrica.

She sighed and then continued, "Such a change."

I nodded. I remembered carrying water skins to the Welshmen who worked on the five foot thick wall. I climbed the cold rectangular blocks of stone and handed up the water skins. And when I was done with that I was busy each day fetching things for the women in the kitchen, helping with feeding the animals, and running errands up and down the hill.

As if she had shared my thought Ulrica said, "Ah, yes, we did work hard. All of us."

She fell silent, and I remembered that rainy day in early April after the Welshmen left. The castle had seemed lonely with only the Saxons who lived here and the Earl's men-at-arms. Lonely, but not boring like today.

"Do you have any errands that need running?" I asked her.

She chuckled and shook her head.

Standing a few feet away, Mother answered, "You can hear the thuds outside, child. No, you may not go out there."

Yes. I heard the thuds of rocks hitting the walls, every one of them. I resented them. They were keeping me from getting outside.

The only excitement that afternoon was when old Wulfstan came to the kitchen. He came in swearing, strange swears about St. Andrew's twisted ankle and Our Lady's long fingernail. He seemed more angry than in pain. Mildred talked to him all the while that Ulrica put ointment and a wrapped bandage over a bruise on his ribs.

"I was up on the tower standing watch and holding a sling pole," he said. "I turned away from the wall for a moment and then I felt hit in the back of the ribs by a rock."

Ulrica and Mildred helped him put his tunic back on and made him sit on the floor where Ulrica had been sitting beside Aethel. He grimaced as he sat down; I worried whether he would be able to raise himself off the floor. Mildred fetched him a mug of ale from the cellar. Ulrica told him to drink the ale slowly and not get up until it was done.

Sitting there silently, he sipped his ale and stared at the oven in front of us with an angry, clenched jaw.

"Great-uncle, do you feel any better?" Aethel asked him.

"A little," he said.

"Has anyone else been hurt?" I asked.

He shook his head no.

Wulfstan gulped the last of the ale and tried to stand. He only rose a few inches off the ground before stopping with a gasp of pain. I ran around to the other side of him, Aethel and I put our hands under each arm. We gently guided him as he raised himself. I thought, *We could never lift him alone. He is a skinny man, but still far too heavy for that.*

With a quiet thank you, he set down his mug and left the kitchen.

"Will he go back on watch?" I asked Aethel.

Aethel said she had no idea.

From inside the kitchen, neither of us had a way to find out.

***

When the afternoon was nearly over, Father came to the kitchen and put his arms around Mother's waist. He said, "Aedrica, get your scissors and a bowl of water."

She gathered them. I realized it was Saturday, the day that the Norman men had a shave and a haircut. Godwin is a good barber, as well as a good blacksmith, and he usually shaved them with a straight razor that he had forged himself. After the shave, Mother gave the Norman men what Mildred called a bowl haircut, because it looked like a bowl had been placed upside down on their heads and then used as a cutting pattern.

"I guess Peter has decided that shaving does not break the ban on bathing," said Rowena.

"I guess so," I said. "We are still getting to wash our hands before meals, but not our faces. Father must have decided shaving was as important as that."

Rowena's older sister Edwina, who had overheard us, said in a waspish tone, "Or making sure they will not be mistaken for bearded Saxon men was more important."

I did not know how to reply to that without starting a fight, so I ran over to Father and asked if I could help Mother. Holding a towel for her would be better than sitting and listening to Edwina. He shook his head and left. I sighed as I watched Ulrica take the five loaves of bread out of the oven. I thought, *Will that be enough for us?* Then I stood up and went over to watch Mildred slice the venison. *Will they really only serve us a slice each? How can we have a meal without fish or eel? We will eat more vegetables than meat tonight. Ughh.*

DAY 4, THE FOURTH SUNDAY AFTER EASTER

I woke with my parents and put on my blue, long-sleeved tunic of wool. This tunic I wore on Sunday, the Sabbath day, and again on wash day afternoons while my weekday tunic was being washed. As I looked at the soil stuck to my under-dress, I wished yesterday had been a washing day.

When I came out of the women's dressing room, Father Cuthbert the priest was dressed already in his off-white wool tunic with a linen tabard over it. Father Cuthbert handed the book of the Gospels to Bert who always held it during mass. Father Cuthbert then marched ahead of us out of the great hall and over to the little altar that had been built quickly out of rocks left over from the wall construction These rocks were too large for the sling pole, so they had been stacked and mudded together by Godwin over the last two days.

The priest started chanting the mass in Latin. I joined in with the others when I was supposed to, but not very enthusiastically. Enthusiasm was difficult, when I did not understand what I was singing. Saying mass out in the castle yard was also distracting. I could hear birds and insects. I could smell grass and animals. I could feel the sun shining on my long brown hair, warming it.

The sunshine was falling on the camp of the King's knights too. Luckily, they were in mass too so they would fire no stones or arrows, and we could all enjoy this morning.

Mother nudged me to pay attention. Father Cuthbert was facing the altar with his back to us, singing the words to bless the bread and wine for communion.

Then he broke the bread so that we could all go up to him to receive a small amount, about the size of my thumbnail. He alone would drink from the chalice.

We all chanted Amen together, then the priest chanted alone and then the mass was done. Father Cuthbert made Bert walk behind him as he walked back to the hall.

I sighed with relief. The mass was over. I was bored, but it was the same sense of boredom that I felt every week, not the boredom of this confinement.

"Rowena?"

She scowled at me. "What?"

"Sabbath means fewer chores. So what shall we do?"

"I am thinking about that. You are interrupting me."

"Oh," I muttered. I sat down quietly, watching the cherry blossoms drop under the cherry tree on the other side of the castle yard. Last week they had been so aromatic and delicate, and now they were starting to rot into the soil.

Rowena crouched down beside me. "I have it. We can get up there this time if we keep our wits. Do what I say and trust me and we will be lucky."

I nodded. "What will we do?"

She peered at me. "The reason we did not get up there before is that we were spotted. So we must not be seen."

My forehead wrinkled. I thought, *How can we do that?*

"Well," she said, "they will see us, but they will not recognize us. We shall get a tunic of your father's for you and one of my father's for me. And two hoods."

I interrupted. "I am much smaller than my father."

"Yes, so am I. But we will not look like Maud and Rowena. That is the important thing. Trust me."

I realized I was holding my breath and forced myself to let the air out.

Rowena was up and walking. I followed.

She walked into the great hall, head held high. She motioned me to stay by the fireplace. She headed into the men's dressing room.

I listened to Sir Jehann at the head table telling

Father Cuthbert and several others about the priest in the village in Normandy where he had grown up. I tried to pay attention, but my hearing was actually focused on the room where Rowena had gone.

I worried, *Is taking a tunic from my father stealing? Even if we put it right back. How much trouble will we be in if this fails? How much if we succeed? Will we have to lie? Father always punishes me worse if I lie.*

Rowena came back out with the wicker laundry basket, half-full of men's tunics and hoods. I followed her out of the hall. No one had noticed us. She headed for the privies behind the great hall.

She set the basket down and smiled triumphantly.

"See, Miss Frightened. It worked. I did not even have to lie. I looked like I was doing an errand, and no one said a thing. You could not have done it. You look white with fear."

I realized my heart was pounding. She was probably right. I probably looked as scared as I felt.

She handed me my father's filthy weekday tunic. My nose was angry. I thought, *Am I going to put this on? Do I want to go on the tower that badly?*

"What are you two doing?" Mildred's voice boomed behind me.

I jumped.

Rowena answered, "Nothing, ma'am."

Mildred opened the door of one of the privies.
"Nothing? Ha! Do you think I was born yesterday? You
stand in front of the privies with a basket of dirty laundry.
I know mischief when I see it. Now, I am going in here.
When I come out, you and the basket will be back in the
hall. You stay in there until I fetch you to help with
dinner."

She pinched my left arm and reached for Rowena.
Rowena slid away and dropped a curtsy all in one move.
Mildred snorted at her, walked into the privy, and closed
the door. Rowena handed me the basket and made me
carry it back.

Rowena sat on the stones of the fireplace. I sat
beside her. Rowena's jaw was clenched, probably fuming
at being caught so early on. I had nothing to say to her. I
was disappointed both in her stinky idea and in it not
working.

***

After dinner, Mildred sent me on an errand to the
horse stable. When I delivered the oats for the horses, I
found Father in the stables, talking to Manfred, the stable
groom, about how much to feed the three light draft
horses. Sir Jehann owned a brown stallion, and Father

owned a bay mare and the mare's yearling bay colt. As castle seneschal, Father was expected to decide the feed amounts.

I walked up to Father and stood at his side patiently like he had told me always to do. When he finished talking to Manfred, he asked me what I wanted. I realized he could never answer all the questions in my head about what will happen when the siege was over, how the siege will end, and when the siege will end.

So instead I asked, "Father, how do you know the Earl will come back for us?"

"Ah, my little girl, the Earl has offended the King and will have to fight to keep his three castles from the Crown," said Father, in his reassuring voice. "The Earl is bound to free all three castles because without these lands Earl Robert is not Earl or rich."

"Please," I went on, "did not the King give this land to the Earl? Is this not the King's land also?"

He looked at me closely and paused before replying, "King Henry claims to have divine right on his side. He claims he has been anointed king by the holy church. He claims this land is his again though he did give it to the Earl. What do we call someone, child, who gives something and then wants it back?"

I also paused before answering. I paused because

my first idea for an answer was little Edric, but I knew Father would not appreciate that joke. Instead I said, "A false giver."

"Exactly. That brings as much dishonor as breaking an oath. Now run along to the kitchen. You should not be out. The rocks could come falling again at any time."

He gave me a nudge on the shoulder, and on my way back to the confinement of the kitchen, I paused to watch one of the four old, brown chickens pecking for insects inside the fenced area around the chicken house. The chickens were penned in, but they were not smart enough to ask why or for how long. Then I looked around for a stick to poke the dirt. I thought, *Maybe poking for insects makes a siege more bearable.*

***

That night as I cleaned the mugs off the tables at the end of supper, I overheard Godwin and Manfred discussing the Earl's army. The brothers were speaking as softly as most of us mutter, standing at the end of their table where they were apart from everyone else in the hall.

"Do you think," asked Manfred, "that they will join the Earl?"

"He has paid for them already," said Godwin.

"Yes. But they are Welsh. Money in the hand has no obligation to them."

I often heard such slurs against the Welsh from the Saxons here at Castle Bridgnorth. Father and the other Normans liked the Welsh much better than the Saxon servants and farmers. Mother said it was because the Saxons had been fighting them far longer. I was not sure. I was not even sure what the Welsh were really like. The only Welshmen I had ever met were the laborers who had worked on the walls this winter. When I carried water to them, they had seemed like sweaty, tired men and not much else.

I walked up closer to Godwin and Manfred. Both brothers were startled. They had not realized I was close enough to hear them.

I decided to be a little bold and asked them, "Why are the Welsh willing to give us an army when they also make raids on us?" I half-knew the answer that this army was coming from the few Welsh princes who supported the Earl, but I wanted to hear what Godwin would say.

Godwin looked at my face. I thought he might be trying to see if I was curious for myself or was going to go tell my father what he said, so I kept my face looking as sincere as I could.

"You know the Welsh princes are all very

different men," he said. "Some respect King Henry, others do not. Some want the land here, and others will stay on the Welsh side of the mountains. A few agree with Earl Robert and will, for money, help against the King. Enough said. Go finish your chores, child."

I thought, *Why do the men and women always call me child when they dismiss my questions?* At the door, I looked back. Manfred and Godwin were now standing there silent, no longer in a mood to chat.

DAY 5, MONDAY

      Mildred had told Aethel, Rowena and me to spend the whole day in the kitchen, partly because the skies looked like rain, and mostly to avoid the stones that I could hear hitting the wall. When the rain started, Mildred had Edwina close the windows on the south wall.

      Rowena whispered in my ear, "The Earl better return soon or I will explode from boredom."

      I nodded whole heartedly. I could not remember the last time that I did not leave this hill for five days.

      We sat down on the floor in the kitchen between Ulrica and Edwina' worktables. I could hear Edwina complaining to Ulrica who was chopping carrots and turnips for dinner, "I do not see why the men are allowed on the watch tower and we are not. Do they think women have no eyes? I can see a stone coming at me. I can duck as well as any man. They have no respect for our ability to handle ourselves. I mean, I have this heavy cleaver in my hands right now slicing the venison for dinner. Do they think it takes no strength to do this? Do they think I am weak? I mean, they come in here all day and watch us working hard all day while they stand up on that tower doing nothing."

      Ulrica broke in with a patient voice, "Did you ask

your father if you could go up?"

Edwina whirled around to face Ulrica, without setting down the sharp cleaver in her hand. "Of course," she replied. "I ask him a couple of times every day. His answer is always no. He says Peter and Sir Jehann have forbidden us and the children from going up there until the stone throwing stops. But I know he agrees with them. Men are all alike. They think holding you back is protecting you."

Ulrica sighed. Rowena rolled her eyes. I had to tighten my face to keep from laughing. This was one of Edwina's common complaints. She was only fifteen and she knew what all men are like even though she had never left this valley and had not met that many men.

I knew better than to remind Edwina that she was only fifteen. I also knew that you had to let Edwina tell you how things are, otherwise she was angry all day.

"I want to see the river again," she continued. "Is that so much to ask? You would think the world was going to end if Father let me have this one thing. I mean, by the love of the Saints, those knights might not even be able to see me up there."

Ulrica warned her to be more careful of the cleaver. The cleaver had nearly hit the table while she was talking and gesturing. That moved Edwina's attention back to work. And I was grateful that it stopped her complaining.

I leaned over to Aethel and whispered that I wanted to climb up there and see the river too. I missed the river Severn and missed sitting on the riverbank with a fishing line.

Aethel nodded, but she admitted quietly that she did not want to climb the tower. The thought of climbing up a thirty-foot ladder rather scared her. I was not surprised; I knew that Aethel never climbed trees.

When Edwina finished chopping the meat, Mildred told Edwina, Rowena and me to go down to the cellar to fill the pitchers with ale for dinner.

I smiled. Filling the pitchers was one of the last chores before serving the midday meal.

Despite my smile, I started trembling as I walked out of the kitchen. I imagined a stone the size of my head coming over the wall and pounding me in the chest before I could move aside. I ran and tried to stop imagining.

The wooden plank cellar door lay on the ground on the south side of the kitchen. As soon as Edwina lifted the door open, we walked down several steps into the cellar that was below the kitchen. Each of us was carrying two pottery pitchers. Rowena was leading the way down the steps, but Edwina quickly stepped around her and took the lead as they walked to the barrels of ale against one wall. The whole wall was lined with barrels stacked three high. Rowena and I held out our pitchers one at a time while Edwina worked the spigot. She always wanted to be the one doing that.

Rowena looked over at the two canvas sacks of ground wheat and five sacks of ground barley lying beside the barrels.

"Are we really going to have enough wheat for bread? What if this siege goes on and on?" she asked.

I looked over at the sacks too. "I have been wondering that too," I said. "When Father brought these back from the miller at Quatford, I asked him how many more he was bringing, and he said this would last until the siege was over. He said we have become used to feeding all those stone cutters. Now that we are the only ones here, it will be enough." I tried to smile reassuringly like Father did.

Edwina's long, blonde hair fell over her shoulder as she laughed.

"My father," she said, "says those Welsh *workers* ate all the Earl's crops, all the grain to be had on the Earl's farms, and this will not be enough for us. I mean, if you look at how much we used only yesterday you would see that my father is right."

I decided not to argue. I had seen how much wheat flour we had used. It did not seem that much. But I could tell Edwina was still mad about not going up the watch tower. I looked over at Rowena who was shaking her head ever so slightly. She did not want me to argue with her either. So we quietly finished filling the pitchers and went back up the stairs.

I made myself walk slowly back to the kitchen. I did not want to spill the ale, and I did not want to let my fear win. I repeated to myself, "The horn will give me warning," over and over.

As the women bustled to load the food on trays, I grabbed Rowena by the elbow and steered her to the kitchen doorway. We might look like we were staying out of the way of our elders.

"Rowena, how are we getting up there?"

She sighed. "My idea yesterday was not very good, was it?"

I shook my head. "The stench was not so good. Maybe we should plan for tomorrow. Today is not going to…"

"Hmm," she said, "Tomorrow. Yes, it might be a lucky day. Let me think about it. I –"

She was interrupted by Mildred calling us to help.

At supper, Rowena nudged Edric with her knee to

make him sit on the other side of her. Then as we ate she spoke softly, explaining in between bites how we could climb the roof of the great hall instead.

"Climb the thatch roof? Are you mad?" I said.

"I am very well set in my mind," she said. "I am also right about this. Think. We have not been able to get on the watch tower. The Maple tree is not high enough to give the view we want, but the great hall is. It slopes to the west and is high enough."

I sat quietly to think about this. The flat planks of the watch tower sounded better than prickly thatch reeds.

Rowena studied my face in the dim candle light. Then she said something to her little brother.

After supper, Sir Jehann stood and signaled that he wanted to speak. I groaned softly, because he could talk forever.

"Men-at-arms, servants, and even you little children," he began in his thick French accent. "Please make of listening to my words. I will speak in the English for you tonight. This will make the words from me more easy to comprehend. Today no stones were thrown at us here in Bridgnorth Castle. I, myself, and William were on the main watch today and we saw no stones large enough to do us harm."

I closed my eyes and tried to think if there were

any large stones over on sheep pasture hill.

"The knights and squires in the army which camps most without reason on the hill beside us have perhaps too much to do today. I was seeing them take a dozen sheep from a local farmer who owes his living to our Earl no doubt, a dozen little sheep butchered and cooked. So they feast well there tonight on mutton we should have use of here in the Earl's castle."

"Also, I saw seven, no perhaps it was eight, new tents pitched for three knights of Mercia, or was it Cumbria, and a score of squires. They were not for servants for they were brightly colored tents, glorious red and others in yellow -"

Father leaned up to Jehann's ear and said something quietly. I could not hear what he said.

Jehann looked down at his plate on the table and paused. Then he looked back up and continued, "Ah yes, I must mention that more knights arrived with squires and the servants. We did not see the Earl's army marching from Shrewsbury by road or river. It makes sense that they should come by the Shrewsbury road, but there are barges that could bring them down the Severn in time much shorter. But that is of no matter, for Peter expects them in a week, while I am expecting them in nine days. Without fail."

I sighed and realized that I had been holding my breath.

"So you should keep in here. Well, not in the hall only, but in the castle buildings. Men-at-arms keep on watch and practice; we must be ready with good training of arms and clean condition of armor when the Earl arrives. Servants keep to do your chores. And I say in expectation that tomorrow should be no stone throwing."

He sat back down, and I heard a sigh of relief from the next table. Rowena, Aethel and I began clearing the dishes off the tables as quietly as we could. The silence in the hall was not the kind I wanted to break, better to let one of the adults break it and be embarrassed.

DAY 6, TUESDAY

After breakfast, Father and mother stood outside the kitchen discussing how safe it was outside. I stood at Mother's elbow, listening both to them and for sounds from over the walls. They agreed to let Edric feed the chickens and let us three girls weed the garden. Mother lifted down four baskets from the hooks. She headed out of the kitchen towards the herb garden which she and Ulrica tended.

On the way to the vegetable garden Rowena said, "I will do the beans today, right?"

"No matter. I will take the carrots," said Aethel.

I glared at Rowena. I was supposed to get the beans today. They were getting tall enough to be clearly recognizable as beans. "Rowena, you had the beans last time. It is my turn."

Rowena looked over at me. My face must have showed the anger I felt.

"Fine," she said. "You take the beans, Miss It-has-to-be-fair."

Rowena reluctantly weeded the turnips, and Aethel weeded the carrots. I was still angry that Rowena had called me a name, and I was willing to bet from her silence that she was upset too.

Aethel was done first yet again. I pulled slowly trying to watch Father come and go from the tower and trying to pull only weeds. I wondered, *Will he be willing to give us permission today?*

After weeding in the garden, we were sitting by the kitchen door watching people working. My father walked by, heading towards the stables. He was scowling. Now was not a good time to ask about climbing the tower.

"It is not so bad today," said Aethel. "The day is getting warmer."

Both Rowena and I nodded. I noticed that the dirt was not cold under my toes. The sun was warming the earth.

We all looked up as Bert came running past us with one hand held up high. I was close enough to the door to see what Bert was doing in the kitchen.

"Ulrica," he said. "I got bit by that nasty sow. Think it needs stitches?"

Ulrica waddled toward him. "Let me look at it. Yes, over here by the window. Mmm. She bit deep. No need for stitches, but you will need a poultice and bandage." Ulrica moved over to the cabinet to get the herbs for the poultice.

Rowena asked me if he was badly hurt. I told her no.

Rowena stood to see around the door frame, and then Edric appeared suddenly, shoved her arm and yelled Tag. All three of us ran after Edric first and caught him by ganging up on him around the Maple tree. Then having tagged him, Rowena was It next. The game of tag went all over the castle yard and had us all out of breath and hungry long before the mid-day dinner was ready.

As we stood catching our breath, Rowena nudged me and pointed at the tower.

"We should go ask to get up there now, right?" she said.

Only her uncle Manfred was up there. I nodded. She and I walked quickly to the base of the tower. We left Aethel and Edric panting back by the cherry tree. We wanted to get there before someone came to join Manfred.

Rowena started climbing the ladder. As soon as her left foot hit the sixth rung, I grabbed hold of the ladder. Rowena kept climbing and was almost at the top, she would be visible to Manfred in one more rung. I was halfway up.

Then I heard Godwin call up loudly below me. "What are you two doing?"

We both stopped climbing. I wondered whether to try telling him that Father had given permission. Then I remembered how badly Father had spanked me for lying at

Christmas. That had been humiliating, as well as painful.

Rowena pleaded with Godwin, "Father, we are only going up for a minute."

"No!" He shouted. "Get back down here!"

We both knew better than to argue, so we climbed down sullenly. When we got to the ground, he shooed us away like small children. As he climbed the ladder, I heard him telling Manfred, leaning over the top of the ladder, how we were sneaking up there.

As soon as we were out of earshot, I said "Why did he have to do that like we were two years old or something? Aargh."

"We will have to make sure he is out of sight next time," she said.

We walked slowly back to the kitchen, where Ulrica was in the doorway holding a basket, watching us with a smirk on her round face. She must have seen the whole thing.

"You may be right about the great hall roof being our best plan," I said.

"I knew you would eventually agree," she said.

***

After supper, I went up to Father at the head table and asked to sit on his lap. His arms were warm, almost compensating for no fire in the fireplace. I listened to Sir Jehann tell him where precisely the Welsh troops were today if they were to be to the castle in five days time. Jehann was certain when the army should be here. I could not understand why he had picked five as the number. At any rate, I enjoyed his description of how the army was a group of men: some archers, some spearmen, and some with swords. All were from four Welsh princes and so would wear many different colors. His story was long and quite entertaining. When Jehann finished, he went over to the table where William was telling a story in French.

I decided this was a good time to ask Father a question. He was relaxed and in a good mood. As seneschal of the castle, he knew the answers to all questions of why things happened. Sometimes he did not answer, but I was certain he knew.

"Father, will we be able to go outside as soon as the Earl arrives?"

He tenderly kissed my forehead and said, "No, my child. A terrible battle will happen when the Earl arrives. The Earl and the army will win the battle and what is left of the King's army will leave. Then you will be free to play outside."

"Oh," I now had even more questions, "then why was Jehann saying the Earl will arrive in precisely five days. If the King's army finds out when the Earl will arrive with his army will the battle not more difficult? I mean, if the King knows the Earl is coming then will the Earl lose his ability to surprise them?"

He laughed. "Jehann is only guessing. It is his way to believe his guess is as good as true. And his guess may be. Now, you are a girl and should not worry about such things. Go clean up supper with the others."

He hoisted me off his lap and set me on my feet. I frowned. That question time was certainly over, and I did not know as much as I wanted. I also believed that if Bert the pig boy could understand battles, then so could I.

DAY 7, WEDNESDAY

The morning was chilly and gloomy, with rain showers and a volley of rocks over the east wall of the castle. When the first rocks landed in the pig pen, the sow understandably squealed in fear. She did not like fist-sized rocks landing beside her and pounding the wooden roof of her shed.

I would rather have been in the great hall, on the west side of the castle. The great hall would have allowed us access to the games chest and the men's gossip. I had suggested it to Father, but he had declared we should be with the women in the kitchen.

Though being confined in the kitchen did have one advantage. From the doorway, I could see Manfred, Godwin and Bert, standing near the east wall, using sling poles, and throwing blindly over the eastern wall of the castle. The tower platform was nearly useless, being over at the northwest corner of the castle.

When a rock volley came in, Wulfstan shot arrows at where he thought the archers were. But not knowing the distance, the arrows probably missed their targets. I heard the sow squeal several more times, and Wulfstan swear when he gave up on the bow, but no noises from the other side of the wall.

Manfred came in from the rain in the early afternoon and stood right up against his wife, Ulrica. He asked for some warm water to drink. He told Rowena and me who were sitting nearby, "I have been throwing rocks for hours without hearing anyone yell in pain. We are simply wasting rocks."

Ulrica whispered some reassuring comment, but he shook his head and sipped some of the water.

"Also I was on the tower earlier," he said, "and I personally saw a group of squires walk into Lord Roger's camp with a score, yes twenty, partridges that they had caught in the river valley."

Rowena was amazed. "Uncle, does the valley have that many partridges?"

Manfred shrugged, but his voice assured her, "The valley has far more than that, but not so close together that you could catch them all in one hunting trip. Squires must have split up and hunted separately."

Mother was stirring something in the cauldron. "You should go tell Peter about the partridges. He will want to know for the Earl's hunting trips this fall."

Manfred nodded to her. He drank his water and left.

I wondered whether the rock throwing would still happen as the Earl and his army march into view. I imagined a couple of squires throwing rocks at the castle on the east side of the hill without stop for days on end and getting so tired that they slept on the hill. And one not waking up and missing the battle altogether and then having to ride back to the King on a cart in shame for having missed the lost battle.

I told Rowena what I had been imagining, and she giggled.

"Maud, could such a luckless squire ever happen?"

Aethel who had overheard me answered her, "You never know. Some people have very bad luck all the time. Like my aunt Gertrude, she never has any good luck."

Edwina who had overheard us spoke up, "I say we are the ones with bad luck, I mean, to be in a castle under siege."

I thought, *Why does she have to spoil the fun of the squire? It was only a story. Maybe though she is right and we are the ones with bad luck. Is bad luck why I cannot get up on that tower?*

I whispered in Rowena's ear. "How can we get up there?"

She shrugged. "We have to get permission for that. I am thinking of a way to get on the great hall roof. Maybe tomorrow, I will think of some way."

I sat quietly and listened to the rest of them talk and watched the men walking back and forth across the castle yard, gathering rocks that had been thrown in. I noticed that only Bert was up on the watch tower. I nudged Rowena and pointed up there.

"Is now," I whispered, "a good time? It is raining, but the rain might hide us. I know you said you will have a plan tomorrow."

She surveyed all around. While we had been standing there, only a few rocks had fallen in. She nodded. "The other men will join him as soon as the east wall is quiet."

We looked at the women in the kitchen. They all had their backs to us. She nodded and ran. I followed her, slower, but still I was there quickly. She was up four rungs on the ladder when I grabbed it. Bert heard us and came to see who was climbing.

"Rowena! What are you doing?" He sounded more amazed than angry.

She spun her head to see him. "I want to get a look. It is safe on this side of the castle today. Please?"

"No! It is not! Get back down there. If you go quickly, I tell no one. Go on."

I had not even started climbing. *No fair*, I thought. Rowena's scowl fit how I felt. We walked slowly back out into the castle yard where the rain had slowed to a few drops.

"How are we going to get up there today, Rowena?"

She laughed. "You sound desperate. Going up there will require more tries, but we can try more, right?"

"Yes. We need help. We need permission."

"How will we get that? No, forget permission."

What she spied over my shoulder made her grin, so I turned to see. Bert was finishing a minor repair on the tower.

"We can get a ladder if we help him put the tools away."

I was still trying to think about what might happen if we forgot about permission. It took me a second to catch up to her as she crossed the yard to Bert.

"May we help you carry the tools back to the shed?" she asked in a too-sweet voice.

Bert grunted and handed her a saw. He gave me a couple of hammers. He hoisted the unused lumber on his shoulder. We trudged back to the shed.

I started to walk faster, but Rowena motioned me back. I thought, *Why should we follow him? If he drops any of the lumber, we will trip on it. Oh, Rowena wants us to be last in the shed. She must be acting on her plan.*

It went exactly as Rowena planned. He dropped the lumber in the middle of the shed and walked off without saying thanks or anything. She grabbed one end of the tall ladder and headed out of the shed. I grabbed the other end and followed.

"Act confident," she said. "Pretend we were told to do this."

I thought, *How do I walk with confidence? Not stumbling takes all my attention.*

No one stopped us. We went around the south side of the great hall and headed for the northwest corner. Rowena abruptly stopped, catching me off guard.

"Here is good," she said. "Those rock throwers are all at the eastern wall. And they sound done for the day."

She tilted her end of the ladder down, and I tilted my end up. The ladder rose more than three feet above the brim of the thatch.

She climbed first and motioned me to follow when she got to the top rung. As I climbed off the ladder, I grabbed hold of some reeds above my head. I tried to stand up but the thatch was slick under my feet.

Rowena was standing above me. I thought, *Had she found some dry thatch?* She motioned for me to stand. I tried to find a foothold without success.

She sighed and headed for the peak of the roof. I

tried to stand again. The heel of my left foot caught on a couple of broken reeds. After a few seconds and a deep breath, I pulled my left knee under my belly and scrambled for a foothold for the right foot.

What I found was a broken reed, which scraped the arch of my right foot. It hurt and I pulled back instinctively, causing my left foot to slip. I was hanging by my hands.

I looked up, hoping to catch Rowena's attention so she would come help me. She was hanging by her hands too, but much closer to the peak.

I heard chuckling from below.

Sir Jehann's voice called up, "Are you making a test of the roof? Are you the apprentices of thatchers?"

Several men laughed.

I tried to release my grip on the reeds in a controlled way, and I tried to aim for the ladder. Luckily Father caught me by the waist as my try failed and I slid feet first off the roof.

He dropped me gently. "My child, what were you doing?" he asked.

"We wanted to see out," I answered as Rowena put her right foot on the top rung of the ladder.

He laughed. The other men, including Rowena's father, Godwin, laughed too.

"If the roof was high enough to see over the walls, a watch platform would be there, would it not?" he said.

I looked down at the sparse grass. I had not thought of that, and neither had Rowena.

DAY 8, THURSDAY

Bert's heavy feet stomped out of the kitchen door as Rowena, Aethel and I were approaching it.

"Aethel," he said grumpily, "I've been told to watch over you three weeding the garden. If I tell you to run, you, Maud and Rowena need to obey me. Hear?" His muscular shoulders were slumped forward.

"I hear," Aethel replied. Her face was a mirror of his. They both had the same unhappy expression at being forced into spending time together.

Rowena and I both nodded when he looked at us for an answer.

Their grandmother Mildred poked her head out of the kitchen and told him, "Get those girls into the garden, boy. Get the weeding done quickly. Rain is moving in."

I looked at the smattering of clouds in the sky. I thought, *How can she predict rain?*

I weeded the cabbages again, Aethel weeded the beans by the wall, and Rowena weeded the beets. Rowena was near where Bert was sitting and watching the top of the wall.

"What new things are happening in the army camp?" Rowena asked him.

Without taking his eyes off the wall, he replied, "I

was on watch yesterday and I counted fifty-one tents. Means there must be more than thirty knights over on that hill. And probably as many squires. And then there will be servants, cooks and washer women. Turning into a proper little town over there."

I was impressed at how many more were there now. Two days earlier, Bert had said there were forty-two tents.

Rowena had stopped weeding, and was now crouching and looking over at him. She asked in a polite voice, "Will there be more coming?"

"Hard to say," he said and then paused to look over at the tower, "Jehann says this is probably all the King will send. But William says if we put up a real fight they might send more."

Hardly any weeds had grown in the last two days of cloudy skies, so I was now done with the cabbages and moved on to the row of turnips. This took me further away from him and his voice. I wished he would speak up a little.

"Are they building catapults or battering rams?" Rowena asked.

"No," he said. "Jehann says they will not bother because they underestimate us. Chrestian says the new stone walls look too thick for a small catapult to do any damage."

"And what do you think?" Rowena asked very sweetly. *Almost too sweetly*, I thought.

Bert scowled at her. He then looked back up at the wall and did not answer.

The weeding was soon done. Mother told us to come inside the kitchen for safety. I groaned softly. Being in the kitchen, close to Mother, gave us no privacy for talking about what Bert had said or Rowena's too sweet tone. It also meant no time to discuss a plan to get permission.

***

After the mid-day dinner, I carried dishes back to the kitchen with the others. We set the dishes in the dry sink, a deep tin bowl resting in a hole in the table top. Edwina poured water over the dishes and cleaned them with a pumice stone and rag. Then she and Ulrica lifted the tin bowl by its handles and carried it outside to empty it.

I set the dishes down as Mildred was handing several long knives to Godwin over by the kitchen door. I heard him say that he would sharpen them and be right back.

I went over and sat down between Mildred's work table and the door. I waved to Rowena and Aethel to join me.

"Why are we sitting here?" Rowena asked. "The floor over by Ulrica has more room, right?"

"Yes, but we can hear Godwin when he comes back from here. We can also talk and plan."

"About what?" Aethel said.

"How to get permission to go up on the tower, silly. What else?" Rowena said.

Aethel shook her head and scooted over a few feet to the other side of Mildred's table.

"Fine," said Rowena. "Then we will go without you, Aethel. I have an idea. You can always get your father in a good mood. He dotes on you. So, you talk sweet to him, sweeter than you did last time, and he agrees to – to let us take a small peek."

"He does not dote on me. He loves me, but he does not show it by giving me what I want. Perhaps I can trick him into giving us permission?"

"We have tried sneaking. Tricking will not be any better, right? You need to sweet talk him."

I stared at the women in the room. Mildred was chopping herbs to go in the venison stew for supper. She had fennel from last summer on the thick, wooden cutting board on her work table. She was cutting the fennel off its branches with a small paring knife that she had not given to Godwin. The fennel released its odor with each cut. I wondered, *Will she help us get permission?*

No. I looked over at Mother who was cleaning dirt off turnips with a dry rag at her work table. *How could I get my mother to help?*

"Aedrica," said Ulrica, "it seems almost amazing that a couple of months ago we were feeding more than two hundred of them stone cutters and stone haulers. We were eight women in this kitchen here, hours before dawn and late into the night every day. So many hours of work for each meal. Now, it will only take four of us a few hours to make each meal for less than a score of mouths. I know I have said it before but I still cannot get over such a quick change."

Mother nodded and gazed out the window over her work table. I thought, I*s she nodding because Ulrica had said that before or because she agrees?*

"That could not have lasted forever," said Mother. "We could not have kept doing that much work much longer. My hands ached from chopping meat and vegetables all day long. And my back. It hurt every night, from standing here all day."

Ulrica nodded as she sat down on a stool. "I hate being confined in these walls by that there army, but it is far less work," she said.

Mother's face tightened the second that Ulrica mentioned the army. I needed to speak now and try to get her to let us see the army ourselves.

Before I could think of what to say she said, "The Earl will be here any day, so we need not talk any more about it."

We all sat there quietly. Mildred looked tired, Ulrica looked disappointed, Mother looked unhappy, Rowena was looking outside, and I had missed my chance. No point to ask now.

Godwin stepped into the kitchen and I could see the knives better now. The five knives, each a different length and width, were used to butcher animals - to cut off hams, bacon, steaks, roasts, and all the other cuts of meat. Mildred thanked Godwin as he set them down on her work table. Then she looked down at the three of us sitting on the floor.

"Do you girls want to come help me? Bert slaughtered the sow this morning."

We all shook our heads no. I had helped with butchering before and knew it was messy work that left me with small cuts on my hands.

"Hmm," she said, "best get your knitting baskets down and work on that."

***

That night at supper, Rowena and I had time and privacy to talk after Edric wolfed down his food and went to sit by his father Godwin. Aethel was still eating, her grandmother having given her an extra helping of bread.

I spoke first. "Do you suppose the King's army underestimates us by thinking that we are disloyal to the Earl?"

Rowena added, "Or that we do not have enough food and water to last?"

Aethel shrugged her shoulders. Her mouth was full of bread.

I thought about the food in the cellar and shook my head no. "Maybe they simply do not know us."

"Maybe we," said Rowena, pointing to herself and me, "do not know us. This might be an easy siege for them to win, right?"

I thought she sounded like Edwina, and to avoid saying that I said, "What do you mean?"

"You know what I mean, but you are Peter's good little girl. You believe whatever he says and do not want to think he might be wrong about us winning."

I took a deep breath. "Rowena, that is not fair. I really dislike it when you accuse me of believing whatever my father says. You know the siege is something my father knows about. He has been in sieges before and he is the seneschal of this castle. So he knows more than me or you."

She shrugged. She did not say anything, no apology. So I changed the subject.

"What about you and Bert?" I asked.

Aethel made a gagging noise which was easy to do with her mouth full of bread, as if the thought of anyone liking her big brother made her stomach twirl.

"Oh, I handled that so badly," Rowena blushed as she confessed. "Did you see how he looked at me? I do not know what comes over me some times. I like him, but I think Edwina does too. And she is older and will marry first. So he will be gone by the time I can marry."

I gave Rowena a knowing look. We knew it was hopeless. Edwina was too sharp for any man to like for a wife. Edwina was doomed to never marry and Rowena might be a spinster. She might not marry until eighteen or nineteen, or some old age like that.

Before I had time to comment about Edwina's chances, Wulfstan stood up at the table in front of us. He began to sing in his baritone voice an old song about a Saxon king who held a fortress against another king and won after a bitter fight. I liked the tune and could whistle along after a couple of verses.

DAY 9, FRIDAY

Aethel, Rowena and I went over to the stable to see the horses. The stable consisted of six stalls and a common area about the size of two stalls. The common area was used for cleaning and caring for a horse.

Rowena's uncle Manfred was brushing the six year old mare in the common area. The mare was tied to an iron ring mounted on the shorter wall as he worked. Manfred was about as tall as the mare at the top of her head. His right hand on the brush worked over the coat on her back. Her back was bowed somewhat from the carts, sleighs and garden plough which she pulled over the years.

Manfred looked up as we came into sight. "Where are the oats?"

"What oats, uncle?" Rowena asked.

"Oh, for goodness sake, you are supposed to go to the kitchen and fetch the horses' share of the oats here every day."

We looked at each other in surprise. No one had told us we had this new chore. I had brought the oats once, but I had thought it was a one-time favor.

Manfred's wiry brown beard jiggled as he chuckled. His laughter made me realize he had been teasing. I started to laugh too.

"Yes," he said. "I am to fetch the oats. But you go do it this morning, Maud."

I grabbed the feed bags off a peg on the wall beside the stable door and ran to the kitchen. When Mildred found me standing in the doorway with the three feedbags, she smiled and walked with me down to the cellar beneath the kitchen.

"Why are you smiling, Mildred?"

She poured three equal measures of oats into the canvas feedbags. "I see Manfred has you talked into one of his chores," she said. "Yesterday he talked Bert into it. That man can talk his way out of more work. If he were a knight in that army out there, we would be surrounded by chipmunks and squirrels doing him a favor."

I laughed.

When I returned to the stable with the feedbags, Manfred was sitting on a bench, letting Rowena brush the mare's legs. Manfred pointed to where I should set the feedbags beside him. When she finished with the mare's legs, he led her back to her stall and brought out her yearling colt. The brown colt was not happy to leave the stall beside his mother, but he knew Manfred and knew not to make a fuss. Manfred led him out to the common area and tied his halter rope to the same iron ring.

Aethel was allowed to brush the colt's coat. She

worked the brush over him quickly, but well. She brought out stray hairs and blades of grass with every long stroke. When Aethel finished, I asked if I could brush the mane.

"Will you brush the tail as well?" asked Manfred.

I nodded yes. He nodded in return, as if he were letting me have a favor.

While I worked the snarls from his coarse brown mane, Aethel sat down beside Manfred on the bench and asked him what he had seen while standing watch earlier that morning.

"Well," he started, "the strawberries in that patch to the west of the gate are nearly ripe. You know, the ones over by the willow tree. The birds were eating some this morning. And a deer was eating some of them too."

Aethel interrupted him, "Are the deer that close by?"

"Yes," he paused to smile, "a doe and her fawn came almost to the gate the other day. Wulfstan told me that he saw a stag grazing right outside the gates. Bold as anything. They must know we cannot go out to hunt. Two weeks ago, that stag would have been hanging in the cellar for coming so close."

"Can we shoot one and drag it in for supper? I love venison," I said.

"Keep your attention on the colt, Maud. We could

shoot it, but we could not risk opening the gates to bring in one deer."

Now Rowena decided to follow that thought. "Why not? No one can run up that steep hill faster than you, and then Wulfstan and a couple others could grab a deer and bring it in."

Manfred's face grew serious. "Peter and Jehann say we cannot know for certain the King's men are all off the hill. Someone could be in the trees at the north end of the hilltop. And those gates do not open so very easily as you think."

I remembered how much work it had been for me and the men to close the gates.

Rowena was ready with another question, "We have not seen anyone over there, have we?"

"No. And they do not leave any trace of having walked on the hilltop. But Peter says there is still a chance. I do not see their chance if we watch them come and go from the army's camp, but I am only the stable groom and not in charge. And neither are you."

Manfred stood up from the bench and walked over to where I was working on the colt's tail. I had found a particularly hard knot of hair. Manfred took the brush from me and told us to leave so he could feed the horses in peace.

"Where should we go?" I asked as we left the stable.

"Back to the kitchen," said Aethel. "Those rocks could pound on us at any time."

Rowena did not answer. She was staring at the stable roof. I stared too. I thought, *What is she looking at? The stable has a wooden plank roof. Nothing to stare at, really.*

"Come on." Aethel said and grabbed my arm.

"You go. We will follow in a minute," I said.

Aethel trudged off, muttering something.

"I see I have been planning all wrong," said Rowena. "We want to see out. We do not have to be by the west wall to do that. The tower and the great hall are not the only way to see out."

"Yes," she said. "We can get up there much easier. All we need is a ladder and we know how to get that, right?"

"Will it be high enough? Those stone walls are tall." I said.

She stared some more. "Yes, it will if we jump. The stable is also far from the northern slope where archers might be. We must try something." The confidence in her voice was enough to tell me that we would be doing this.

"Can we get a ladder? I mean, I think they will not ignore us walking around with a ladder this time."

She shrugged.

How, I thought, *will we see the army from the south wall? Before the wall was there we could see the river and the valley from there. Maybe I should ask her before she makes a plan to fetch the ladder.*

The horn on the watch tower sounded twice. Incoming rocks or arrows. Rowena and I started walking back to the kitchen while watching the west wall.

Edwina was standing at the kitchen door with our orders. "Rowena come help chop turnips. Maud, Aedrica says you and Aethel are to go get your knitting and practice.

"Knitting again?" I moaned.

Aethel, who had been sitting on the ground nearby, looked at me with a frown on her lips and forehead. "I enjoy knitting," she said.

"Why? Because we sit in one place?" I said.

"No," Aethel replied seriously as she grabbed her needles and yarn from the basket. "I like the way the wooden needles click and slide against each other. And I like how the rows look like there are many pieces of yarn when there is only one."

I nodded. I did like the look of a big knitted

stocking, when it was done. But I could not agree with actually enjoying making it.

I worked with the needles until I noticed that the heap of wool in my lap felt and almost had the weight of a kitten. I closed my eyes until they were slits, and I could barely see the wool. I started to pet my woolen kitten, along the back. It felt soft and warm.

The illusion was broken when Aethel laughed. "What are you doing?"

I closed my eyes all the way and set my hands down on the wool. "Pretending I have a kitten in my lap."

"But that is not a proper kitten doll. Grandmother made me a cuddly puppy doll out of wool when I was little. That is a lump of wool."

"I know that. I was only – never mind."

I sighed and opened my eyes. Rowena was trying not to laugh out loud, but I could see her shoulders shaking over at Edwina's work table. Aethel had gone back to knitting, or maybe she had never stopped. I went back to knitting too, now with my heart aching to actually pet a kitten.

DAY 10, SATURDAY

Mother, in her soft blue wool tunic with each sleeve rolled up precisely three times, was busy sweeping the kitchen floor. I came into the kitchen to get the weeding baskets. I stopped with the baskets in my hands.

"Mother, why do the gardens have to be weeded three days a week this year when last year once a week was enough? I know we need weeds to help add to our meals, but why so often? The weeds are getting shorter and shorter because we are weeding so often."

She looked up from sweeping, fixing an irritated gaze on me. "We need the weeds for food *now*. If we leave them the hares might get them."

"But we do not want the hares to starve, do we?"

Instead of answering me, she said in a too quiet, angry tone, "Go outside and do not ask again."

I knew that tone ended all discussion of the matter. She went back to sweeping, and I trudged outside with the three baskets. I tried to figure out how having a few more weeds in the food was more important than the hares. *Everyone knows the hares have the ability to bring a good harvest. And the harvest must be important when we have so little food stored. Life in Bridgnorth makes no sense this summer.*

As I worked my way down the row of carrots that were barely sprouting out recognizably, I realized that I had not seen a hare, or even a little rabbit, since I had last been outside these walls. I stopped looking for weeds and looked up at the thick limestone wall. I thought, *What hare can hop through that? And with the gates shut, they certainly can not get in.* Last year when there had only been a short wooden fence around these buildings, I had shooed hares out of the garden at least once a day.

***

Later, we found Edric by the stable. He had a metal hoop that had fallen off a large rain barrel. The barrel could not be fixed until it was taken to the cooper in Shrewsbury after the siege. Until then it was ours for playing.

We played a game of hoops and sticks. Rowena was quite good at this game. She could get the hoop rolling and keep it rolling by prodding it very gently with a long stick. She rolled it on as flat a piece of ground as possible and prodded it so lightly that it did not fall over.

After winning twice, Rowena claimed that she was not better at this; she had simply had more practice. I doubted that. I had almost the same amount of practice as her and could not keep the hoop upright for more than ten feet.

Rowena started the hoop going again. I looked down at my arms and noticed how dirty they were. My hands went to my hair, greasy and sticky. This day should have been a bathing day. I looked up at Rowena's hair, blowing in the wind as she ran. It looked every bit as dirty. We were combing our hair each morning, but combing is not as good as bathing.

I thought, *Will I bathe as soon as the Earl's army gets here? That might be a few days.*

***

After playing in the castle yard, we were all thirsty. So we went to the kitchen and begged for some water. Mother took us to the water barrel and let us drink from a ladle until we felt like we might not need to eat dinner.

Mother walked with us over to the watch tower and called out to Father, who was on watch with William.

"Peter, how are things going today?" she asked.

He leaned over the tower and looked surprised to see that we were all standing there with her. "Children, there may be more rock throwing. The King's men were out hunting this morning. They have returned now. So they may make some mischief. Go inside for the rest of the day."

Mother gave him a sour look. "Peter, they want some chores to keep busy or some news to chat about. I know perfectly well how dangerous it is out here. I will not let them come to harm this morning."

He leaned even further over the railing and smiled, easing his facial muscles. "They are bored, eh? As for news, ten squires and two knights brought back four bucks and one doe from hunting. Yesterday, they caught two bucks. So there goes my work of three years letting the bucks in the herd mature and grow full-antlered."

He continued, "As for chores, Edric go help your father in the smithy. Girls, go help in the kitchen. Good enough, my dear?" He pulled himself up straight, out of my view.

Mother escorted Edric to the smithy and pointed us back to the kitchen. Once in the kitchen, Rowena and Aethel went to sit by Ulrica's work table and sat cross-legged, facing each other. I tried to follow them, but Mother came in and put a steering hand on my shoulder and led me to the right corner of her own work table.

Rowena started a clapping/rhyming game that required both players to say rhymes to the beat of the clap, each trying to speak it right as long as possible.

"Maud, you will help with chopping," she said.

"You like having something to do and twelve is old enough to be helping. Surely, you have had enough of sitting on the floor in here?"

I watched them longingly and sighed.

The table had a mound of parsnips on the left. Mother stood in front of the parsnips and began peeling each yellow vegetable. The peels went into a bowl, a bowl to be carried to the animals.

As she finished peeling each one, she handed it to me who then chopped it into thick coins. I could hear them on the other side of the room.

"I am going by road to Winchester,

I am going by road to Chichester,

I am going by road to Rochester"

I wished I could be over there. She must have read my mind.

"Maud, is it not better to be busy here doing good work?"

"Yes, Mother."

She chuckled and kept on peeling. I thought, *Is she enjoying my discomfort?* When the pile was done, Aethel moved over and I took her place in the game. Edwina had taught this rhyme about going to town to see a merchant to Rowena and me a couple of years ago. We both knew it by heart. We clapped the rhythm, slow at first, but then building as neither one of us missed any of the rhyme. We were speeding up again, when a thud and a crack came from outside. Rowena and I stopped in mid-clap, startled at exactly the same time.

Everyone in the kitchen ran to the doorway to see what had made the noise. A triangular piece of wooden plank and a large stone were lying beside the watch tower. The stone had hit the watch tower roof and then toppled to the ground.

Another stone hit the roof and stopped on the tower platform. Sir Jehann bent over, seized that same stone and fired it from a sling pole.

Edwina stepped through the doorway and out onto the path to get a better view, away from the thatch overhang. Mildred grabbed her arm and used Edwina as a prod to get the others to move back into the kitchen. "We have plenty to do in here and no business out there," she said. "Get back to work."

Rowena and I whispered "No Fair" in unison, and then we laughed in unison. We stayed near the doorway. We had no work to do. Aethel, however, followed her grandmother to the oven to help her there. I thought, *Why did Aethel not want to see the rocks coming in? This is exciting in a scary way.*

The stones slowed down after a few minutes. I

heard Sir Jehann yell in French, "Ha! They like that not at all!"

"Rowena," I asked quietly, "do you think we won that round?"

She shrugged.

"Where do you suppose the army is throwing from?" I asked. "Some of these stones are the size of a goose egg. Could they come all the way from the sheep pasture hill?"

Rowena pointed at the tower. "If we could get up there, we could see for ourselves."

Mildred, now standing at her work table, answered both of us. "You girls are definitely not going up there. Neither am I. However, Bert has and he tells me they stand lower on this hill behind bushes and have some contraption – oh, what did he call it – well anyway – they have some thing they put rocks in and shoot them up here. Like a crossbow, only stronger."

I said a polite and heart-felt thank you. At least someone knew and was willing to tell me.

Rowena nudged me, and I looked outside again. Wulfstan and Bert were cutting smaller boards out of the plank that had fallen. Godwin walked up with another large plank, slightly larger than the one that had broken. Bert then took a pouch of nails from Godwin and put it on his leather belt. He grabbed the boards and started to climb up the ladder. He climbed out over the platform and up onto the roof.

Luckily he was on this side of the tower where we could watch him.

He laid the large board over the hole and used the small boards to hold it in place. I thought, *A rather shabby patch. Will the men go back up there and repair the roof better after the siege?*

"We should follow them to get a ladder," whispered Rowena.

"I heard that," said Mildred. "You two are doing no such thing. You will stay in my sight all day if that is what it takes."

DAY II, THE FIFTH SUNDAY AFTER EASTER

I stood with every one else in the cool morning air in my Sabbath dress. My fingernails were following the thread in the dark blue embroidery on the cuffs of my left sleeve, while Father Cuthbert was saying the mass. I was trying unsuccessfully to hear the Severn River beyond the walls and down the hill.

My mind supplied the sound of the river that I could not quite hear. I followed the base of the hill around to the east where King Henry had scores of men, maybe hundreds of men, camped on the hill. Maybe the troops had ground all the grass and brush from the land. Maybe it was now a desert, like the one Our Lord was tempted in. I had never seen a picture of a desert, but the priest said that deserts were a terrible place where no plants grew and where heathens lived.

I wondered what exactly a heathen looked like. I had never seen pictures of one. I wondered, *Perhaps they look like the Welsh. They are short and slightly dark-skinned. They dress strangely. Were heathens even more different looking than that?*

Mother nudged me and I started paying attention again to words of the mass which I knew by heart, even though I did not understand the Latin.

As I walked away after mass, I put my hand in his and looked up into his calm face. "Father, can Rowena and I go up on the wall to see the river?"

I did not mention wanting to see the King's army. I knew that was the wrong way to ask.

He suddenly stopped walking and gazed up at the tower.

"That is not possible."

There was kindness in his brown eyes, so I decided to push the issue, "Please, Father, I want to see the river. It has been so long, almost a fortnight since we were down by the river, please."

His eyebrows grew sterner.

"Absolutely not," he said. "The men-at-arms are up there on watch and do not want distractions. Besides, my dear, the King has archers."

"But the tower is safer than the roof of the great hall?" I broke in.

The skin around his eyes constricted. I knew that he was not going to give in. I had said the wrong thing. I could imagine that he was thinking of Wulfstan who had been wounded on the tower by a stone. I started to open my mouth to say but that was days ago. I started, but then I recognized the look he was giving me.

I quit the attempt and went off to find Aethel and

Rowena. Maybe we could play a game of nine man's morris in the great hall.

***

We ended up going to a sunny corner of the garden, under the young, wild cherry tree. Sunshine always beats being stuck in a gloomy room. On the way there, Aethel stopped by the great hall to pick up the wooden nine man's morris board and the colored leather playing pieces. Nine for each side.

Because Aethel had retrieved the board, she was to be one of the players in the first game. As Rowena and I walked into the garden and over to the tree, we argued about who would play Aethel. Stopping a few heart beats short of name calling, I won.

Aethel and I laid the board on the ground, chose colors and started laying down pieces, one per turn at the intersections and corners.

Meanwhile, Rowena sat back against one of the immense stones of the wall to watch the game. She watched the game intently until the fourth move when she could see I had grabbed three really important intersections. Rowena watched the birds flying nearby. They were a pair of willow warblers, both males. Their dark brown, speckled wings were flapping as they flew, but they were not singing.

Rowena broke the silence of the game, "Maud, what did your father say about us going up on the wall for a look?"

I thought, *Has Rowena's bird watching made her desire for freedom from the castle only worse? Or is she bored? Or is she feeling lucky about getting to see?*

"I am trying to play this game," I said firmly, trying not to lose my concentration.

Rowena went back impatiently to watching the warblers.

In nine man's morris, the placement of pieces in the first few moves determines who will have the high ground for the rest of the game. Aethel had forgotten this and thoughtlessly put her second and fourth leather coins down in bad places, which gave me the win.

Before Rowena's knee could nudge Aethel's body out of place at the board to play the next round, Aethel looked me in the eyes and asked how the question to my father had gone.

I broke the eye contact, looked down at my dress and said, "He said no."

"Why?" they both asked at once.

"He said it was too dangerous."

"Did you tell him we cannot remember what the

river is like?" said Rowena.

I nodded sadly.

After a second of quiet, Aethel asked, "You told him you will be very careful and you will only be sticking your heads over the top for a second and..."

"Aethel," I said, "you said you did not want to go up there. Why are you asking?"

"I simply want you to get your way so this adventure is at an end," she said.

I dropped the leather pieces I had been picking up off the board. "Adventure? Wanting to see the enemy outside is not an adventure. We have to know what is going on there."

Rowena plunged on, ignoring Aethel's insult of our intent. "Did you tell him we will only glance and come right down?"

"I did not get a chance. He gave me that My Word is Law look."

"Oh, and you cannot ever try to change his mind, can you?" said Rowena.

I went back to picking up pieces. "You know how my father is, Rowena. He does not move once he has made up his mind."

"If you were a Saxon, you would know how important it is to be able to see your enemy."

"Hey, you know Maud is both Saxon and Norman, so leave her alone," said Aethel.

Rowena threw her hand up over her left ear; she was not in the mood to hear it.

I came to my own defense. "I am a Saxon."

She picked up her game pieces casually. "Maud is a Norman name. You are exactly like your Norman father. Whatever he says you do."

"My mother is a Saxon, and you do whatever your father tells you to do. And you believe everything he says. So why do you tease me?"

"Do you suppose," said Aethel, "that because we have no way out maybe the army will be leaving? I mean, if we have to stay in here and wait for the Earl, maybe they could let some of the knights go home? I think I will ask great-uncle Wulfstan if they are really all still there. He said last night that the army was getting larger by a few tents every day, but maybe some will leave today."

Rowena and I laughed. I stopped laughing when I could see we had hurt Aethel's feelings. I said in my kindest voice, "I wondered something like that too, but Father says that is not how it works. We are trapped in here because they are a large army. If they let knights go home, we will be free to attack what is left of the army."

I looked over at the tower. Then Rowena nudged

my foot and pointed at the board. Time to start the game.

I lost, and to make the day worse, Edric came running up during the next game. "I get to go on the tower, I get to go on the tower," he chanted.

Rowena accused her little brother of lying. He stuck out his tongue.

"Tomorrow," he said. "With Father and Uncle Manfred. You will see."

Then he ran off as quickly as he had run up. *Probably gone off to tell someone else his good news*, I thought. Rowena and I finished that game with very little enthusiasm and then put the game pieces back in the games chest in the hall.

As we left the great hall, Rowena leaned close to me and said, "If that little idiot gets up on the tower tomorrow so will we. And if that fails, we will be on the stable roof by sunset. I mean it."

I nodded. I could see no reason not to agree with her.

DAY 12, MONDAY

Edric was inside the base of the tower playing with rocks when Rowena and I arrived. He nearly exploded with joy and giggles when Manfred and Godwin arrived shortly afterwards for their turn at standing watch.

I could see that Edric had no intention of cleaning up the rocks he had tossed around, so I started to stack them again. Rowena joined me and asked her father if she could go up too.

"I told you last night," said Godwin. "No. Your brother is going to be only up there for a few minutes. And it is no place for girls."

I thought, *Why are all the exciting things only for boys?*

Rowena gave her father a sweet, pleading look, but it did not work.

Godwin's iron-strong hands gripped the ladder. Edric scrambled up after him. Father and Wulfstan came down the ladder. Their watch was over.

I caught Father's attention. "May I go up with you some time, father?"

He glared at me. "No. Godwin is foolish taking his little boy up there. Get out of the tower."

We left the tower, but did not go far. We walked

down the rows of the vegetable garden far enough to see Edric up in Manfred's arms. He and his uncle were looking out over the wall at the army on the hill opposite. Manfred was pointing over in the army camp. Godwin was facing south, watching over the castle to the Severn River Valley. None of them were looking north across the hilltop.

"He is not going to be there only a few minutes," complained Rowena. "That little whiner is going to be up there all day, I bet."

I did not reply. I did not know if she was right.

A few minutes later Aethel said she wanted to sit down. So she wandered back to the spot by the kitchen door.

Edric's voice drifted down to us; he was saying something to Manfred.

And then he was not. He was out of Manfred's arms. Manfred and Godwin both screamed his name at the top of their lungs. All the men in the castle came running. Rowena and I came running too, right over the vegetables.

Manfred started throwing stones out over the wall to the north, pelting the rocks with fury. Godwin was hopping down the ladder with his back to the rungs and Edric in his arms.

Rowena and I were close enough to see what had

happened to Edric. A crossbow bolt was in his chest, above his heart. Blood was everywhere. He was not breathing. He was dead.

I had seen dead people before. I had been there when my mother's mother, Grandmother Aethelhild, had died of a fever two years ago. I had also seen the body of Rowena's mother, who had died having a baby three years ago. But this was different. Blood was dripping, and it was Edric. Pesky Edric.

Aethel had come running and was now at my side. Rowena followed her father and brother back to the great hall. I did not go with her; I felt anchored to the ground by useless legs.

Edwina came running and screaming out of the kitchen, heading for the hall as well.

Ulrica bustled out of the kitchen with a large bowl of water and strips of cloth and herbs. I wondered if she thought he was only hurt.

Sir Jehann and Chrestian grabbed the sling pole and headed up the ladder. I heard the men signaling each other as they started loading and releasing the sling pole.

The sight of the sling poles swishing finally released my legs. More crossbow bolts would soon be shot in here. I moved towards the hall and followed the crowd walking there. As I approached the great hall, I turned back and looked up at the tower. The look on the men's faces was terrible. If they had been trying to hurt the King's knights before, they were now trying to kill them.

In the hall, Aethel was lighting candles on the tables so that everyone could see. Edric was laid out on a table which had been moved to the center of the hall near the fireplace. Father Cuthbert was leaning over the boy saying prayers for him. Ulrica had given up hope of curing him and was sitting on a bench crying and holding a sobbing Rowena. Godwin was gray-faced, standing by the little boy's feet. He was oblivious to his oldest daughter, Edwina, sobbing on the ground beside him.

Mildred and Mother came into the hall with another bowl of water and a few cloths. As soon as Father Cuthbert stood back, they started to clean Edric. They were crying too. They kept moving though, even with the tears streaming down their faces.

I realized I was crying too. I felt useless and terrible. I had felt so jealous of him less than an hour ago. And now I wanted nothing to do with that tower.

I will not ask to go up there again, I thought. Father came to stand beside me. He put his arm around my shoulders, and I put my head on his chest. I could hear his heart beat. *I do not want him to risk his life and go up there either.*

"Will someone be so good as to go fetch Edric's good tunic from the men's dressing room?" Mother asked.

Godwin motioned that he would go. He was in the dressing room for a long while. He finally returned with Edric's sky blue woolen tunic. When Mildred and Mother put it on Edric, the sleeves came up the arms a fair way. He had almost outgrown the tunic.

Once Edric was dressed, everyone started moving around looking for chores to do. Aethel and I followed Father back to the stable where Wulfstan and Bert were standing.

Father had focused all his attention on Wulfstan. "Go fetch logs and build a pyre for the boy. That is your Saxon way."

Wulfstan stared questioningly at him a moment. "We have not done that since the days of heroes and Saxon gods. Has Father Cuthbert said to do that?"

I touched his arm very gently. "Father, where will he be buried?"

He ignored me and answered Wulfstan, "I am in charge here. The priest will do as I say."

I backed away from him a step, as Father Cuthbert came trotting up. He must have heard my father speaking. Bert also backed away.

My father greeted Father Cuthbert, "We have no

consecrated ground here at all. Plus, the soil is thin on the rock. So we must build a pyre for the boy."

The priest's face tensed. "We have to bury the child. He must have a grave to rise from on the last day. No, Peter, his immortal soul rests on this."

"We shall set him in the cellar until this siege is over, then," said Father. "The Earl should be back within a week."

Godwin marched up with Bert and Manfred in tow. His face was set like a statue.

"What are you going to do with my Edric?" asked Godwin.

"The soil is not deep enough to bury him in here, plus the ground is not consecrated. We will build a pyre in the Old Saxon way or set him in the cellar until the siege has ended."

I crept back up to his side. I wondered, *How does he not have a plan for burying people in here? Father always has plans for what to do.*

"That boy's body will rot down there. In winter, you could do that. But now – the food will catch the stench," said Wulfstan.

Father Cuthbert interrupted, "But we must wait until he can have a burial. A decent Christian burial."

I tugged on his right sleeve. He looked down at

me. His temper had tightened his lips. "You could wait," I said, "until the middle of the night, then quietly open the gates, then Godwin and Father Cuthbert could quietly carry out Edric and then they could bury him in St. Leonard's churchyard."

I smiled with pride at having solved this problem.

His face only snarled. "What?!" He exploded, and my smile vanished. "In the still of the night that gate opening could be heard for miles. There is no quietly here. We now know they have men on the hilltop. You would only get the smith and the priest killed. Be quiet."

He faced Wulfstan, and I slunk back to where Aethel was standing by Bert.

"Build a pyre like I told you, Wulfstan. Father Cuthbert," he said still looking at Wulfstan. "you say a funeral mass over the boy's body. Godwin, you have my apology. Proper burials do not always happen in war." His solemn face said that he was now done speaking.

Godwin looked about ready to explode. Wulfstan must have seen it too.

Wulfstan put his arm around Godwin's shoulders. "Edric died of a battle wound," he said. "He deserves the funeral of an ancient Saxon hero. God will understand, yes?"

Godwin glared at the cobblestones.

Father Cuthbert spun on his heel and marched off.

I approached Father again. He was not smiling, but he was no longer angry at us all.

"What if they left at dusk, when the world is still full of sound? That is not the still of the night." I asked.

He grabbed me by the arms. His fingers dug into my bones. He steered me backwards towards the Maple tree. His face came down to mine. His nostrils hardened. "Do not ever question me like that again! Not ever. I will not beat you, this time."

He let go and stomped off, following the priest.

Aethel ran over to hug me, and I cried on her shoulder. I thought, *Why can I not ever seem to come up with the right answers? Why is Father so angry that I tried to solve this? His solution was certainly no better. Do Wulfstan and Father Cuthbert feel as defeated by my father as I do?*

Bert came over and told us to go in the kitchen or great hall. More fear of rocks.

Aethel and I sat in the kitchen for what seemed like days. At one point I went to the doorway when I heard Father's voice. He was speaking to the men over by the base of the tower. I wandered out in the castle yard so I could hear him.

"What I feared has happened," he said in his

commanding tone. "The army was able to get a few archers up on the hilltop within range of shooting. We had hoped that if they remained over on the hill opposite, out of range they could use no archery. I have made it clear to Sir Jehann and he agrees that keeping the army from getting up on the hilltop again is most important. If they can go there at their pleasure, they could use flaming arrows or a battering ram on the gates."

He concluded, "When you stand watch, keep your eyes open to all directions and shout at the slightest movement up the hill. Better to alarm at a deer than to let them get an advantage."

I thought, *What could stop the rocks and arrows? Perhaps Rowena is right and this army will kill us all.*

***

The funeral was that evening. We had eaten some slices of barley bread and cups of ale while standing in the castle yard. I had never eaten standing up like that before that I could remember. No one seemed to be hungry. Father Cuthbert said a mass for Edric at the stone altar. The castle was silent except for the priest's voice. Sir Jehann and William, who were standing watch, had stopped the exchange of rocks an hour before to lessen the chance of a rock landing in the castle yard during the funeral.

When the somber mass was over, the priest stayed kneeling at the altar. We all walked back to the cobblestone area between Godwin's smithy and the stable. A large pile of wood had been placed on the cobblestones for the pyre. I heard Mildred who was standing behind me mutter to Bert that he should have been buried outside the castle walls. Bert muttered back that Peter made the choice.

Godwin, Manfred, my father and Wulfstan lifted a plank with Edric's body up onto the pyre. His arms were stiff at his side.

I could not stand it. I could not watch. I turned away and looked at the Field Maple tree behind Mildred. At the whoosh of the fire being lit, my tears started flowing again. I thought, T*his is the Old Saxon way. Will the smoke carry his spirit up to the heavens?*

Mother put her arms around me. She was faced forward, strong enough to look. I stayed there a long time with my cheekbone nestled against her collar bone. Eventually, the heat of the fire was no longer as warm on my back.

After the fire had burned all the wood to ash and charcoal, we started moving in to the hall. Without being told, the men moved the mattresses into place for sleeping.

DAY 13, TUESDAY

Aethel and I weeded the vegetable garden alone. Rowena and her sister Edwina were crying, sitting on the floor, when I brought in my basket of weeds for sorting.

When I returned from taking weeds to the stable, Rowena was now learning how to work the butter churn. Mildred was patiently standing behind her, showing Rowena how to move her arms up and down, showing her the speed and rhythm of moving the churn.

My mouth fell open slightly. Mother saw me and whispered that Rowena had asked if she could help. She actually *asked* for a chore. However, she was not smiling and was not enjoying herself. So she must still be herself somewhere deep down.

When the churning was done Rowena went over to a corner and sat crying. I sat beside her and tried to talk to her a few times, but Rowena shook her head and gestured that I should go away. Aethel and I did go outside again. We went over to the southern wall of the kitchen and watched Manfred exercising the stallion. When an arrow landed in the grass, Father, who had also been watching, ordered us into the kitchen for the rest of the day.

The afternoon went slowly. Rowena spent much

of it crying. So did Edwina, but not together in the same corner.

Aethel and I were not in the mood for knitting or games. There was very little talk to overhear as no men came in and all the women were quiet. So they left me alone to think. *If Father is right and our men must keep the King's men off the hill at all costs, how will they do that? The sling poles are most effective from the tower, but from there they can only really reach down the western and northern slopes of the hill. So how will they keep men off the eastern and southern slopes?* I thought of all the weapons that I had seen in the castle. Nothing came to mind. *Why have they not built watch towers all along the wall?* Finally, I realized that was due to lack of time. It had been April before they had started building this watch tower.

Then, my mind starting torturing me by creating images of crossbow bolts coming over the walls and hitting everyone in the chest, like Edric, as we all walked about the castle yard.

I had a hard time seeing the floor for tears in my eyes. I closed my eyes, and tears slipped down my cheeks. But when the images of crossbow bolts appeared, I opened my eyes again. Mother came over to me. She held me silently, until the tears stopped enough to see again.

"Maud, dear, will you be all right if I go back to cooking? Be a big girl and do not cry any more. Crying does no good."

I nodded and Mother stood up.

Aethel who had watched me crying went to fetch the knitting basket. "We might not be in the mood for knitting, but you like doing something."

***

Supper that night consisted of roast pork sliced thinly and roasted turnips in gravy. Everyone ate quietly. The absence of a plate and mug for Edric was a reminder of our loss.

The bench in front of us scraped across the floor. Wulfstan's long, silver braid and beard stood out in the candlelight of the hall against his blue wool tunic as he approached the fireplace. He began to sing a beautiful, sad song of a young man who chases a goddess across a bog and can not walk on the bog as the goddess does. Father Cuthbert stood up the first time Wulfstan's song mentioned the pagan word goddess, but William sitting beside him pulled him back down onto the bench and whispered something in his ear. The priest relaxed, with a sour look on his face.

By the end of the song, everyone was crying,

partly for the young man and partly for Edric. When Wulfstan sat back down everyone, except Father Cuthbert, stood up and clapped. I wondered, *How can he keep from crying when the song is so sad?*

DAY 14, WEDNESDAY

Before mid-day, Father called us all to the castle yard. He had his reassuring face on.

"We have not seen the Earl's army yet this morning," he said. "Earl Robert will keep his promise and be here with an army of loyal Welsh to raise the siege within fourteen nights of the army's arrival. The Earl is certain to be here soon, in the next few days."

I thought, *Is the Earl to be here within a fortnight of his leaving or the army arriving? Did he say leaving days ago and now change it?* I stared at him as he finished speaking.

"However, we must go without a midday dinner for a few days until the Earl arrives and we can go hunt for food."

I thought, *Is he telling the truth? Will the Earl be here today?* Father looked like he was telling the truth, at least as far as he knew it to be true. I smiled at him and hoped he was right.

***

As the day wore on, Rowena did not volunteer for chores. Instead she sat over near Edwina at her work table and did not speak to anyone. I volunteered for errands to the stable or great hall.

On a trip to deliver the horses' oats to the stable, I smelled lilacs and sniffed after them like a hunting dog finds the direction of prey. I realized I was smelling the lilac bushes beyond the west wall. I wished that I could go gather the beautiful blooms.

Gloomy rain moved in at midday, and I was not as eager to run errands in the slightly cold rain. So I sat quietly all afternoon, listening to the women talking.

"Seeing these food scraps," said Ulrica, "reminds me of a fierce cat on my father's farm when I was a girl. That cat, we called her Blackie, had the ability to scare large cows away with one hiss. No really, that cat raised her hackles and made this hiss that sounded like a whole group of cats at once. Blackie once birthed a litter of kittens right in the cow's stall of the barn and was able to keep them safe until they were grown by keeping the cow huddled on one side of the stall at night."

"Are we the cats and the King's army is the cow?" I whispered to Aethel.

"I do not know," replied Aethel. Aethel's face grew sad. "That is not a very happy idea."

I was about to say sorry for making her sad, when Mildred started in with a description of the blooming apple trees that Bert had spotted down the road by St. Leonard's

Church while on watch. It sounded so lovely. I remembered climbing one of those trees before the siege.

***

In the somber candle light during supper, Father had sad eyes. So as soon as I finished my food, I went up to the head table to try to cheer him with a hug. He stood and we hugged, and then he addressed the others who were eating.

"Tomorrow, Earl Robert will hopefully return. If he has not arrived by tomorrow afternoon, we will slaughter the milk cow."

Several people gasped. Mother's brown eyes grew more severe.

I wondered, *How will I eat porridge without cream?*

His gaze went around the room and his eyes brightened. "I refuse to kill the horses and the four chickens," he said. "The horses will be needed when the Earl's army arrives. The hens produce eggs. We will dine on beef until our good liege Earl Robert comes to raise this siege in a couple of days. There will be food aplenty until then. In addition to beef, Mildred and the other cooks will serve fine meals picked daily from the gardens. We will also feast on birds that even the King cannot keep from flying over this castle."

He sat down with a reassuring smile. I smiled back. I noticed several adults were smiling too. Father could do that, could make people smile back or could make them afraid when he scowled.

I sat down at the children's table. I stared at my empty plate and wondered how many more animals would be slaughtered and whether Father had actually planned for enough food.

Then Rowena asked me how long I thought this siege would go on.

I shrugged. I honestly did not know. "I hope it will end before we run out of beef," I said. "I hate the idea of salad for supper." I hoped to get a chuckle from her on that comment.

Rowena simply nodded and stared at her plate.

DAY 15, THURSDAY

Today was the day Earl Robert was expected by Sir Jehann and Father to return with an army. Before breakfast I heard the clop of horse hooves on the road outside, but the watch on the tower did not sound the horn to welcome the Earl.

Carrying the breakfast bowls back to the kitchen, I heard Aethel gasp. I followed her gaze at the garden. An arrow shaft was sticking up out of the row of carrots near where we were walking. I nearly dropped the bowls, and then grasped them too hard.

Sir Jehann, on watch duty, yelled down to us all, "More arrows will be soon hitting the wall. Those despicable knights are using squires and men-at-arms with crossbows and Saxon bows to fire arrows up from the trees over there at the northern slope at the top of the wall here by the useful vegetable garden. All you, the women, must to stay indoors."

I ran for the kitchen as fast as the pile of bowls in my arms allowed. Not to heed Jehann, but from my own fear at the sight of the arrow.

Mother gazed out from the kitchen doorway. When Father came by, she waved to him and he came to her. They spoke softly and I could not hear the words, but

I could hear that they were using their loving voices.

When he left she smiled and said, "Peter has agreed to us working on fleeces in the great hall. He says the men are all busy repelling the archers and practicing with weapons. So the hall is ours."

***

I sat on the dirt floor by the fireplace in the great hall helping with the weaving and sewing. There was no fire today, but it was safe from arrows and bolts.

The washing, dyeing and drying of the fleeces had been done in April outside near the pig pen. Once dry, the fleeces were carried into the cellar to dry and await carding and spinning. On most afternoons in the fall and winter for as many years as I could remember, little children played on the floor, young women like Rowena and me sat on the floor cleaning and carding the whole fleeces, and grown women sat facing each other on benches spinning, weaving and knitting.

Today, Mildred sat over near the door at the loom. She had learned to weave with my grandmother Aethelhild, who was Mildred's aunt, when they were little girls.

As I sat down, I was thankful that at least the army had not shown up until after the spring fleecing on the

Earl's sheep farms. This helped to keep boredom away on this day at least. My task was to take the yellow-white wool and tease it with the brushes, called cards. This cleaned it of thistles and grass, and I softly molded it so that it could be spun. As I sat near Mother's feet, I liked to watch the drop spindle hang in mid-air between her left hand and the floor. The pile of wool in her lap became a strand in her right hand and then worked its way down onto the spindle.

"Mother," I said, "when will the men slaughter the milk cow?"

She gave me a sad smile, "We will make a venison soup from the deer bones today. Mildred thought of that. We will give the cow until tomorrow. Maybe, she will not be slaughtered at all."

I looked up from the carding brushes.

Edwina spoke, "Aedrica, your husband may be the seneschal, but you have to admit the Earl was stupid to take on King Henry."

"I do not have to admit any such thing," Mother answered. "I am sure the Earl would not have brought this siege down on us without a sincere belief that Robert of Normandy has the divine right to be a better king. I am sure as soon as the Earl arrives with his army he will set things right."

Mildred's head nodded in approval at what Mother had said, but Ulrica and Edwina looked disapproving.

Ulrica, who was also spinning said, "It does not matter who started this argument. King Henry may take this place and we may all be dead by the hands of his knights."

"Absolutely not!" Mother retorted. "The King will not breach these strong stone walls and the men-at-arms will hold here until the Earl arrives." I could see her face was getting flushed, a sure sign of anger. Unfortunately, Edwina did not know the warning signs of her temper as well as I did.

"Aedrica," said Edwina in a persistent tone, "I mean, the Earl has had more than two weeks to show up with an army and he has not."

Now she had done it. I scuttled quickly to the side to make way for Mother who jumped up and started pacing the room.

"He will! How dare you doubt him! What adder nest did you slither from? If I hear such terrible, vicious lies come out of your mouth again, I will... By Our Lady, I will cut your tongue out with a paring knife!"

With that, she paced out of the hall towards the little stone altar which had been set up at the east corner of the castle wall. Before the siege, she calmed down by taking long walks up and down the hill. But now that those stone walls were in place praying at the little stone altar would have to suffice.

Her threat did stop the talking. Edwina looked like she had no intention of ever talking again.

I finished carding the wool in my lap. Then I gave the balls of wool to Ulrica and walked over to the stone altar.

"Mother," I said, "you know she was simply talking. Will you really punish her?"

She sighed and gave me a shoulder hug. "No, dear, but if we start to talk about the siege like that, we will give in faster. At least, that is what your father says. He has been under siege before."

"Oh," I said. "Do you think the Earl and his army will be here soon? I want to know. I will not tell the others."

She laughed. I thought, *Now what had I said funny? I did not mean to make her laugh.*

"The others would hear though," she said. "No matter. I truly believe he will, Maud. The Earl paid four chests of gold for these walls. He will not let this castle with his precious new walls go to King Henry. The Earl values gold far too much to let the rents from this land go to another lord."

"Were those the chests those Welshmen loaded up last September? I remember wondering why they had so many guards for some baggage," I said.

She nodded and walked me back to the kitchen where Ulrica had started working on supper.

***

During supper, I heard Aethel talking to her grandmother who had come over to our table to give Aethel a bit of her watery venison soup.

"Grandmother," Aethel began in her polite voice. I realized she was about to ask for something if she used the polite voice. "What do the men do here in the hall all day while we are in the kitchen?"

Mildred smiled at her and replied, "From what I seen and from what Bert and Wulfstan tell me, they sit talking and playing games. Much the same as you girls." Then she added, "Only talking of different things, mind you."

I could see Aethel was now ready to ask for whatever it was.

"May I bring the men their mugs of ale tomorrow?"

I thought, *Oh, Aethel is a bright one. If she brings the mugs she can stay and hear what they are saying about the army camp, about the Earl's return and all the exciting things they must talk about in here. I wish I had thought of that idea.*

Mildred stared at Aethel a moment. Then she answered, "You do not usually ask for chores. Especially ones that require heavy lifting. No, you may not go listen in on the men's chatter. You leave that chore to Ulrica."

I could hear her old lady chuckle when she got back to her table and told Ulrica what Aethel had said.

As we cleared away the supper plates, I told Aethel that I liked the idea and that we should keep working on that tomorrow. She nodded.

DAY 16, FRIDAY

I woke up before dawn to the sound of a loud crash. As I woke, I tried to tell if it was a boulder hitting the castle wall or thunder. I heard it again, definitely a crash of thunder. I lay there relieved, listening to the storm for well over an hour. The storm settled into a steady rain by the time breakfast was ready.

I did not enjoy carrying the bowls of porridge on trays between the kitchen and hall that morning. The tray was becoming slick from the rain drops. The porridge was becoming watered down and cold. The path between the slippery, wet stepping stones was a string of mud puddles. By the time I got to the hall, gobs of cold mud were wedged between my toes. I tried scraping my feet on the grass, which took off the top inch but left a muddy under-layer.

As I walked into the hall I nearly slipped where the rain had made the stone threshold slick.

After I delivered the bowls, I walked past the fireplace. No fire was there to warm me. We all sat shivering while we ate the now-cold porridge. I really missed not being able to run to the river. I thought, *How joyous it will be to clean my feet in the river again.*

I could see my parents and Sir Jehann at the high

table speaking excitedly about something. My father went over to William and told him the news. *Was the Earl's army here?* I could see the news spreading down the tables. Aethel overheard Bert and Manfred talking, and she relayed the message to Rowena and me.

"Grandmother says this rain will go on for hours," she said. "The men are planning to shower out in the rain. They will wash their tunics in the rain too. Then they will have a fire in here to warm themselves and dry off their tunics. And the women will have to stay indoors in the kitchen all day."

I was instantly saddened by the thought of another day stuck in the kitchen. I had been drenched this morning, but no one had built me a fire to dry off. I was filthy too. I could feel the heavy mud on the hem of my tunic. I had not bathed in a tub or the river in weeks. It did not seem fair.

I was still frowning when I dropped the dirty bowls on the board beside the dry sink in the kitchen. Aethel and Rowena did not look happy either.

Aethel grinned suddenly. "At least we will not be able to smell my brother from the other side of the castle."

Mildred who was standing near us laughed and slapped Aethel's hand for impertinence. She then repeated Aethel's saying to Mother who was a few feet away.

Mother came over and gave me a hug. "Why do you look so glum, dear?"

"Mother, I want a bath too. And I do not want to be in here all day. And I want to know when the Earl will be here."

I looked at my ankles and feet. They were dirtier than I had ever seen them, even dirtier than after helping Manfred sweep out the stables. Mother followed my gaze.

"I understand. We all want to go outside, and we all want the Earl to arrive today. We must have patience, dear."

She continued, "I think we all want a bath. Ulrica and I set the bath tub out beside the herb garden early this morning. We shall see if it fills before the rain ends. If it does, then we may bathe also. We should be thankful for what we can do, and we should notice others. The men do need a bath, very badly. They have been doing animal chores and training exercises this whole time. Mildred and I will need a bath when we get done butchering the cow."

I nodded politely at her to show I had heard what she said. Then I fetched our knitting basket from the cabinet. Aethel and I started to work again on our socks. We had both finished the first sock and were now working on the second one. Aethel's second sock was turning out almost the same size as her first sock. Mine was far larger than the first. I thought, *How much practice will I need to make a pair?*

Mildred and Mother did not stay in the kitchen to work; they went out in the rain to the cobblestones to butcher the milk cow that Bert had slaughtered.

By the time the rain ended in the early afternoon, the bath tub was nearly full. Edwina stood her ground when Mildred asked her and Ulrica to go carry the tub into the kitchen.

"Why should I go lift that heavy tub?" Edwina whined. "I can barely stand for grieving my little Edric. I should go ask my father to lift it."

Ulrica sighed and motioned to her to come. They walked around the herb garden to where the tub was sitting. The tub was slightly wider than a rain barrel but only half as deep. Ulrica grabbed the far handle with both hands and Edina grabbed the nearest one. They carried the heavy tub only a few inches off the ground to the kitchen, stopping several times for a rest. When they lugged it into the kitchen, they set it down only a few inches past the door.

While they had been carrying the tub, Mother had gone to the great hall to fetch washcloths, the soap which the men were now done with, and our good Sabbath tunics.

"Ugh," I whispered to Aethel. "We missed our chance to go into the hall and overhear what the men were talking about."

Aethel looked at me strangely. "Why do you want to go listen to the men? They will either tell us what we hear in the kitchen or they will try to frighten us."

"It was your idea yesterday," I said.

Aethel's face cleared. "Oh, that. That was yesterday. I only want to get clean today."

I bit my tongue to avoid saying something mean about Aethel's poor memory. I decided to ask Rowena if she wanted to sneak into the great hall.

Mildred had told us girls to get stripped down to our sleeveless under-dresses. I even took off my wooden cross. Hair was to be washed first. Mildred bent Aethel over the tub and lathered her hair. Then Mother did the same for me, the lovely smell of soap replacing the smell of grease and dirt.

Edwina beckoned Rowena to come, but Rowena declared she would do it herself. Edwina made a humph noise and stood aside. I washed my own arms, neck and legs. I thought it felt wonderful, almost as good as bathing in the river on a hot day.

Once we were done, the older women stripped down to their under-dresses and washed, while we sat on stools by the oven to dry off in our cleaner, Sabbath tunics.

Mother and Mildred scrubbed our filthy tunics in the now dirt brown water. They rubbed soap against the woolen cloth and dunked the tunics to rinse them as best they could.

Mildred told me and Ulrica to take the pile of woolens outside to the wash line to hang dry. The wash line is set to Mildred's height so I only had to reach up a little. After a while, Mother brought them the men's tunics from the hall to hang as well. When she joined us, I still had a smile on my face from being clean and being outside.

DAY 17, SATURDAY

Rowena was in the kitchen. She had said she was not in the mood to play with us, so only Aethel and I were sitting on the fence around the pig pen. We were pretending the feeding trough was a pond. We were fishing in the pond with the poles, lines and hooks that I had not used since that day the siege had started.

I reeled in and called out, "Whoa! That fish was huge and it nearly bit the hook."

Aethel nodded. She kept her gaze on the pond looking for fish bubbles. Every time she spotted one, she moved the line over to that area.

As I sank my line back in the pond, both of us were startled by a male willow warbler that flew right at us and landed on the fence post a few feet away. He had beautiful dark brown wings.

"Did you fly over the high wall, little bird?" I asked him softly.

Aethel chuckled softly. "Do you expect it to answer?"

"No," I said. "But I can talk to him anyway. He has seen the hillside today and I wish I could fly like him."

The sound of my voice startled the bird and he flew off towards the Maple tree. He flew from branch to branch in the tree, higher and higher. Finally he rested on a branch hanging over the stable for awhile and flew down to the stable roof. He flew up the roof in short bursts and away over the wall.

Aethel went to put away the fishing gear, and I wandered over to the Maple tree. I took hold of the lowest branch, about chest high. My plan was to climb the same branch as the bird and leap to the stable roof and hop up on the wall. I thought, *I can carry out Rowena's plan for her. There is no time to go get her now. Will I be seen? Probably. Will they try to stop me? Hard to say.*

My legs wrapped around the branch. I reached over and grabbed a handful of bark to steady myself on the trunk. Then I grabbed for the next branch. *How long has it been since I last climbed this tree? Keep thinking about what I am doing.*

The next branch was higher than the last, so I focused on getting my right leg up onto the branch. Reaching around the trunk, I stretched my neck for a better view. *I am not far enough up to see over the wall yet. How many more branches?* I glanced up.

"Are you crazy? You are not a bird," Aethel yelled up to me.

I sighed and kept slowly shifting my weight around the trunk to grab the next branch.

Father's voice bellowed from below, "Maud! Come down here!"

From the sound of his voice, he was not below me. I craned my neck to see him, and my right grip loosened on the bark. I tried to grab the branch again and missed. My left hand had nothing to grip.

I fell.

Luckily, I landed on my feet and behind. He set me on my feet and grabbed me by the shoulders. His face clouded over.

"Child! What were you doing?"

"Trying to climb the tree to see out, Father," I said, working to keep tears from forming.

"What? That will do no good. Why can you not understand? You must not try to see out. You are to wait patiently, like a good girl would. Are you too simple to be a good girl?"

A horn sounded, and I was saved from more of his angry words. He let go of me and ran for the watch tower.

I was breathing heavily but not from climbing or falling. I was angry at him for calling me simple-minded for being curious. *Does he want us all to wait here like rocks until the Earl rides in?* I thought.

The horn sounded again, and I realized it was not our bull's horn on the watch tower. This sound was lower and had come from outside the castle walls. I grabbed Aethel's right hand and ran for the western wall, through the row of turnips in the garden.

Aethel and I were alone at the wall. Most of the people were near the tower, the kitchen, or the gate. Father and Sir Jehann were climbing the ladder in the tower. Godwin and Bert were already on the tower platform.

"Why did you do that?" asked Aethel.

"The Maple tree," I answered. "I was trying to get on the stable roof like the Warbler had and then get up on the wall. To see out, and if I could get down on the other side, I might be able to run to the Earl and tell him to hurry."

Why did I tell her that? She is my cousin, but not my protective friend. Now, she will tell the others or make fun of me herself, I thought.

Aethel looked like she wanted to say more, but she closed her mouth. At least she did not laugh.

Godwin called out from above, "Several knights on horses are riding up the hill. Flying a flag. They want to speak. I now count twelve riders."

The men on the tower did not have the sling poles with them. Bert climbed down to make room for Sir Jehann and Father. Horse hooves were pounding on the path. *The first ones must be by the gates now*, I thought.

Aethel tugged at my hand and gestured that we should go closer to the gates. We started tip-toeing very carefully through the garden. More horses were coming up the path. After what I thought was the sound of the last horse stopping, their horn sounded again, even louder now that it was up on the hilltop.

A young man's voice called out in French. He was yelling loudly and gave a long speech of which I could only make out a few words. As soon as he finished, another young man's voice started speaking in English. I supposed it was the same speech spoken again for the Saxons in the castle.

"Men and women of Bridgnorth, King Henry and Lord Roger de Montgomery wish you to hear this. Robert of Belesme who until this winter was Earl of these lands is under siege at Shrewsbury. He has no means to lift this siege. The King will be victorious here. Tell your Norman seneschal that you do not wish to starve. If you surrender, the King and Lord Roger will be merciful. You are without a lord. You are Saxons. You know that you need a lord as much as you need family and home. The King himself will provide for you. We do not look for you to answer this today. Speak with your Norman seneschal. Think of your duty to your King."

When the voice stopped yelling, I heard the horses

move back down the path. They did not wait for an answer.

I looked at Mother over by the kitchen. Her look was stern. I thought, *She must not be in favor of surrender.* Edwina was asking her something. Judging by Edwina's posture, the question must have been spoken gently. Mother looked at her and sighed. Mildred said something and pushed Rowena and all the women back into the kitchen. Then Mildred pointed at Aethel and me and motioned for us to come to her.

Rowena, Edwina and Ulrica were sitting on the floor over by the oven. I followed Aethel over and joined them.

"Stay in here, in case of trouble," said Mildred.

Aethel hugged her and asked, "Grandmother, what kind of trouble?"

Mildred ignored her.

"But supper is already in the pot cooking," said Edwina. "There is not much for us to do. The sunshine is so lovely out today."

Mother did not reply in words. Instead she went over to the cabinet and grabbed the basket of yarn and knitting needles. She brought the basket over and set it down between us.

I decided to take a risk with her. I asked as politely

and gently as I could, "Mother, does this mean the siege will be over tomorrow?"

Mother's face hardened with anger, but then she paused, took deep breath and answered, "Not unless the Earl's army arrives. We will wait patiently and the Earl will be here soon enough. Your father told me so himself this morning."

I knew better than to ask any more of the questions bothering me. *Why have the King's men chosen today to give their speeches? In what way will the King be merciful? Is it true that the Earl is trapped in Shrewsbury like we are trapped here?*

I tried to concentrate on the stitches in this row. It did not work. I did two good stitches and then I looked up at the kitchen window, wondering if I dare ask another question, wondering if I dare to ask her to help me find a way up on the wall.

***

Supper that night was quiet. Much more quiet than usual. I whispered to Rowena and asked her if she knew why. Rowena only put her finger to her lips to gesture that I should be quiet. When I stared at her, she shrugged.

I thought the roast beef was good enough, but there was not enough. So the quiet could not be that people were that busy eating. Even Sir Jehann was quiet.

I asked Rowena what she thought of me trying to get on the stable roof.

Rowena was playing with her spoon. "Is that what you were trying to do?" she said.

I nodded. "Why not go that way? Less work than trying to steal a ladder."

She shook her head. "Jumping from the tree to the roof is a bad idea, Maud. Not even the squirrels make that jump. The ladder will work better. But I will not help you. It is not safe to see out. It only leads to…" Tears kept her from finishing.

I scooted down the bench to comfort her with a hug.

At the end of the meal, my father stood up and asked Father Cuthbert to lead us all in a prayer for the Earl and his army to have good weather for marching to Bridgnorth. Then he produced a friendly smile. Father Cuthbert's prayer in Latin went on for several minutes and at the end we all said amen.

DAY 18, THE SIXTH SUNDAY AFTER EASTER

Aethel and I were playing tic-tac-toe with a stick, drawing the Xs and Os in the wet dirt under the Maple tree. Rain during the night had made the ground moist and easy to make lines in with the stick. Our hands were getting dirty, but we were sitting on our heels carefully to protect our Sabbath tunics from mud. We feared Mildred yelling at us for that.

Sabbath mass had ended an hour earlier, and we had no chores until supper was ready to be served. Rowena was in the kitchen again, staring at the floor and crying once in awhile. I had not even bothered to ask if she wanted to come out and play.

"Ha! I won again," said Aethel. As she spoke she twisted a strand of her dirty hair around her finger. I realized my hair must look every bit as dirty. I remembered how nice it had felt after I had washed my hair earlier in the week. If only I could braid the hair back, but I must keep my hair loose as a maiden should. I minded that rule less when I could wash in the river whenever I felt like it.

My attention came back to the game.

"Yes, that makes eight so far today, two for you and six for me." I paused before speaking again, "Do you remember what Edwina said about men being so much more allowed to do things?"

"When did she say that?"

"Oh," I said. "Days ago, maybe a week ago." I tried to remember which day she had said it. The confinement of the siege was making the days slide together in my memory.

"You mean that day she was so angry at not being allowed to go up the watch tower?"

"Yes. Do you think she was right? Are the men stronger than women or do they think they are? I mean, we are told not to go outside when rocks are falling and we are told not to go up on the tower."

Aethel interrupted, "But little Edric died up there. It is dangerous!"

"I know that! What I mean is my father and your brother and great-uncle face that danger, so why may we not face it too?"

"Grandmother tells me that when she was little," said Aethel, staring at the stick, "before the Normans came to this part of England, things were different. She says her mother owned livestock in her own name."

"Really?"

"Yes." She nodded.

Now I was silent. I thought, *Owning some geese*

or sheep is not the same thing as being as strong as a man. But does it mean women can do more than Normans like the Earl or Father let us?

"Rules for women do not apply to us anyway," I said. "We are still children according to Saxon or Norman law. We will not get to walk about unless we are being guarded."

"Yes," she said. She drew a winning O.

"Aethel, would you want to be a man? Well, if we could?"

Aethel stared over at the stable where Manfred was cleaning the harness leather. "No," she said. "I like little babies. I think I will like being a mother."

I imagined her holding a baby. "I think you will too," I said. The flat rock in my hand was useful to clear the game board.

I thought, *Why can I not be a woman, yet still have as much right to know what is going on as Bert or Chrestian or any of the older men?*

We went back to playing tic-tac-toe. The only noise in the castle yard was from the chickens clucking in the hen house.

After a few rounds of tic-tac-toe, we heard the horn. Father was pointing south from the tower platform. Where he pointed, a large flock of geese were flying towards the castle. I counted fourteen.

William and Chrestian ran up, carrying their crossbows and quivers of bolts. As soon as William found a position for firing, he kneeled on one knee and pulled a bolt out of the quiver and notched it on the crossbow, sighted the flock, and pulled the trigger. He missed. He had another bolt notched quickly. Chrestian took a second longer to shoot; the bird was nearly overhead. He hit it. He also notched another bolt.

William's second shot hit a bird as it passed over the north wall and descended on the other side of the wall. I went to fetch Chrestian's bird. It had fallen by the little stone altar. Chrestian beckoned me to follow him to the kitchen where he presented it to Mildred.

Aethel wandered over when I left the kitchen. "That was exciting. Do you think we will all have some goose tonight?" she asked.

I looked back up in the sky to the south. "Not unless more fly over. That goose will only feed a few people and you and I will not be one of the few."

***

I was right. That night at supper, the head table and the table where Chrestian, William, and Father Cuthbert sat had roast goose.

I was also wrong. At the end of meal, Mother motioned to me to come up front to the head table. After I bobbed my head respectfully to her and father, she told me to hold out my hand. I smiled as she put half of her slice of goose in my hand. To me, it tasted more delicious than anything I had eaten in the last week. I realized I had nearly forgotten how good roasted fowl tastes.

I curtsied, thanked her and went back to my table, quite happy to have been wrong when Mother was right.

DAY 19, MONDAY

Our breakfast porridge was cold from being carried through cold morning drizzle. I noticed that Rowena was eating more slowly than everyone else.

"Are you feeling well enough to weed in the rain?" I asked her.

Puzzled, she stared at me. "I feel fine," she said.

"Oh," I replied. "You are eating so slowly that I thought you might be sick."

She stared at her wooden spoon that was halfway to her mouth. "Eating without him is so lonely and..."

I thought, *Poor Rowena. What can I say to that? How can I cheer someone who has a right to be sad?* "You will need food today so that you can do chores," I said.

Rowena shrugged.

I went back to my own bowl, almost empty now. When I ate the last spoonful, Rowena shoved her own bowl in front of me.

"No, you need that," I refused.

"Eat it," she insisted. "It must not go to waste. I have no appetite for it."

I tried to catch her eye, so I could force her to take the bowl back. But Rowena knew me too well and got up from the table. I ate the porridge. Between the two bowls I almost had as large a portion as I ate before the siege. I ate it ungratefully; mad at Rowena for how I had been given it.

When I was done, I helped gather the bowls. Rowena had already taken a stack to the kitchen. I smiled at her, and she smiled back.

"I will be all right now that the meal is over," she said.

"Several of the herbs are now ready," said Mother, "so today we will have a change."

As Aethel was walking out of the kitchen with her weeding basket, Mother motioned for Aethel to come with her. Slightly jealous, I saw them go to the herb garden over by the kitchen door. Mother always harvested the herbs herself, and she had already brought in the dill which was hanging in fragrant gray-green bunches from the ceiling in the kitchen. As I started on the row of carrots, Aethel was weeding where the dill plants had been. Mother was resting on her heels, carefully gathering one of the other herbs.

I started at one end of the row of carrots and Rowena at the other end. We met well past the mid-point. Rowena was taking time to pull each weed slowly and time to pause between weeds, even more slowly than I do. I thought, *Is her not eating breakfast robbing her of swiftness?*

We went back to the kitchen and met Aethel outside the door. Mother was at her work table sniffing at large bouquets of freshly cut fennel that she had tied. Mildred sorted the weeds for Rowena and me.

After weeding, Rowena went to sit in a corner. I wanted to go to help at the stables so that I could judge how hard it was going be to climb up on the stable roof. I knew Rowena did not approve, but I wanted to try anyway.

Aethel said she wanted to lay in the castle yard and stare at the puffy, gray clouds.

Rowena must have realized why I wanted to go to the stable. She insisted I go with Aethel and threatened to tell my mother why I really wanted to go to the stable if I did not go with her.

Aethel led me by the hand over to the grassy spot near the base of the tower where we looked at clouds passing overhead. When I spotted Father Cuthbert starting the noon mass at the small altar, I whispered to Aethel that we should go back quickly to the kitchen before the priest wanted us to attend mass.

We sat by the kitchen door waiting until the priest finished his mass. A few minutes later, William walked into the kitchen with two graylag geese. He was followed by Chrestian carrying a gander and a goose. The gander had darker feathers and was almost twice as big as the smallest goose.

Mildred took two geese from William and thanked him in her formal voice. Mother took a goose and gander from Chrestian and asked who had shot them.

"These two are of mine," he replied in his poor English. "The gander is of my brother. The other goose is of Wulfstan. Jehann on the tower tells to us that another flock is flying from the south. We are running for our crossbows and arrows. Wulfstan he has one of your Saxon bows. This time we are aiming before the flock is over the south wall. And here they are. They will taste good, no?"

"Very good," replied Mildred.

The men left the kitchen. Mildred, Edwina and I took the birds outside to the cellar entrance where we plucked the birds and collected the feathers in a sack for repairing or making pillows. Mildred and I did most of the plucking, as Edwina was having trouble with her fingers. At least that is what she claimed.

When I came back to the kitchen, Ulrica was kneading barley bread dough.

"The carving knife," she gasped. "It must be sharpened before we cut those geese. Maud, go get it there on the table. Yes, that one and take it to Godwin for sharpening."

Coming close to the doorway of the smithy, I heard male voices arguing inside. I decided not to go in. Instead I crouched down on my heels beside the door, out of view to anyone inside. I carefully laid the knife down in the dirt.

From there I could tell Godwin and Wulfstan were arguing.

"I did not say you were," said Wulfstan.

"Yes, you did," said Godwin.

"No, I said it does not matter if we agree or not. We have sworn an oath of fealty to the Earl. Whether we like it or not we have to go along with it."

"I did not swear an oath and neither did Manfred," said Godwin in his most angry voice. "Only you men-at-arms are important enough to make an oath. Us, servants, we simply say yes when asked if we intend to work here the rest of our lives."

"Oh, well, I swore an oath and you did not. But still you had better not let Peter hear you saying that there is no honor in a siege. He will think the worse of you for it and it will not do any good. That is my point."

I sucked in my breath. Wulfstan sounded closer.

"And my point has nothing to do with honor," said Godwin in a calmer voice. "How do we know who is right with all this hiding behind walls? We need two armies to fight it out. We will probably lose, but then they will be right and we can get on with living."

"Godwin, you said this all winter. I heard you then and I hear the same thing now. If only Earl Robert had put that gold into buying an army instead of buying castle walls. I know it is the Saxon way. What I have been saying to you for months and you do not seem to get through your thick skull is that Normans do not see it that way. They think sieges are proper warfare. For them, battles are to lift sieges or hold higher ground. Last summer in Normandy, I was there when the Earl and many knights besieged two castles. I swear to you that is what they do."

"Sieges! Sieges! Sieges! I am fed up! I make arrow heads here and when will I make swords? I ask you that. Swords are for war, not sling poles."

"Listen. We lost the war against the Normans when I was a young lad - before you were even born. This land is not ours to say how to wage war," Wulfstan said. "We are merely servants. Be careful Peter does not hear you."

"May Peter have a week of bad bowels! I care not what he hears."

I clapped my hands over my mouth to keep from gasping.

"You should remember he is your better," said Wulfstan. "I have to go now. You calm down."

I scurried over to the fence of the pig pen.

Wulfstan came out of the smithy and walked over to where I was now leaning leisurely on the top rail of the fence with the knife loose in my hands.

"You heard us?" He leaned on the fence too.

I nodded. "Some of it."

Wulfstan looked into my eyes. "Please do not tell your father or mother. Godwin's grief is coming out in bitterness. He will do his duty to the Earl when it comes to it. Wager on that."

I nodded again. Though I was not sure I agreed. Godwin had griped all winter against the Earl's plans.

"Good girl." He patted me lightly on the shoulder blade and walked off towards the stable.

I stayed on the fence until I heard him stop clanging a hammer in the smithy. I did not want Godwin's temper to still be red-hot when I took the knife to him.

***

Predictably, the head table for supper had goose liver pate, half of the roast gander, some roast beef, and barley bread. The other tables had roast goose, small portions of roast beef and barley bread. The filling, tasty

153

supper improved moods. People even laughed when heavy rains started pounding on the thatch roof half-way through supper. At the end of supper, Father asked Manfred to sing "The Silly Goose".

The song was one I knew well. Manfred sang it at most goose feasts. In the first verse, a goose is silly and flies too high, far too high. He put out his arms like wings during that verse.

In the second verse, the goose turns over in the sky as she gets close to the sun and her breast feathers are singed. Then Manfred clutched his chest and made funny faces as if he had burned himself. In the third verse the goose tries to cool herself in ponds, lakes, and even puddles. Then Manfred squatted down like a goose floating on water, with his arms tucked under his armpits like wings. As he finished the song, he began to honk like a goose. Everyone laughed, and Ulrica complained she was married to the silliest goose ever.

DAY 20, TUESDAY

Mother looked at Aethel, Rowena and me, tut-
tutted at our filthy arms and hands and announced that the
onions were ready to start harvesting. Ulrica would show
us how to dig up the onions, which given the muddy state
of the garden would surely leave us filthy.

Ulrica took us to the cow shed to fetch a flat-
edged shovel. Then we all walked back to the garden. She
took the shovel and planted it down in the ground beside
the onion at the end of the row.

"Now watch me. Plant the shovel far enough out
to avoid the bulb of the onion, but not so far that you dig
up unnecessary dirt. I will bring up the first one and then
you will take turns with the others. That way you all work
and get equally muddy. We need ten onions today."

She dug the onion out on three sides. Once she had
it out, she tossed it to the grass at the end of the row. She
walked up to Rowena and handed her the shovel.

"I have done this before. But last year we let them
get big and tasty," said Rowena.

"Mmm," Ulrica nodded as she replied to herself
more than to us. "Well, this year we will have them young
and small. I am told in Normandy and Picardy they like
onions this way. Did you know Picardy is someplace over

the channel by Normandy? Mmm, Wulfstan told me that."

Rowena did a good job and soon had an onion to toss beside Ulrica's. Then she gave the shovel to me.

I had not dug up onions before, so it took me five shovel loads. A great deal of dirt came out too. Luckily, the onion came out in one piece.

Aethel grimaced as she planted the shovel down in. She was not as strong and it took all her weight standing on the shovel blade to get the shovel to go down into the soil. She did finally get an onion out too.

"Are the Norman knights over in the camp eating onions?" I asked Ulrica.

Ulrica sighed and her face grew sad. "Oh child, they are eating everything. I really feel sorrow for my father and all the Earl's farms in the valley. Those farmers are almost certainly being made to feed the army. And then my father who owns that hill on which they are camped, he will not be able to use it for pasture. Of course, he may not have any young sheep left to graze on the pasture. The knights and squires and servants will be eating the grain from last year, the livestock, the garden crops, the honey, the deer, and the wild birds. "

"Will the King pay the farmers?" I asked.

She laughed a sad laugh. "What you children say amazes me. It really does." she paused before speaking again. "No. The King will consider taking the crops and livestock part of punishment for the Earl. And even if the Earl was still in the King's favor and this was just a visit, he would expect the Earl to give him all this. Our Norman king does not pay us Saxons."

As we had now harvested ten onions, Ulrica told me to clean the shovel and put it back in the cow shed. Aethel and Ulrica gathered up the onions and carried them to the kitchen. Rowena sat down in the grass right there at the end of the row. She stared down at the new holes in the garden until I came back from the cow shed and escorted her back to the kitchen to clean the onions and ourselves.

Mildred had set out one wide-rimmed clay bowl of cold water for the three of us and three wash cloths. Mother scrubbed me hard with soap on the face, arms and legs. Then Mildred scrubbed Aethel, and then Edwina scrubbed Rowena. We had to sit on a stool to dry off without getting dirty again. At the end of the bath, the water was as brown as beef soup stock.

Once we were dry, I could see that it was becoming warm and sunny outside. This day was too nice to be in the kitchen. Perhaps no stones or arrows would spoil it. I went to the great hall and fetched the nine man's morris board and stones and met Aethel over at a sunny spot near the base of the tower. Rowena followed us, but was not in the mood to play or talk.

Aethel played the first two moves well and won the first game. I had the advantage as the loser of starting the next game; the advantage was enough and I won. As we started a third game, I heard a dog barking outside the gate.

I called out to Manfred and Bert who were standing watch, "Whose dog is out there?"

Bert leaned over the railing on the tower platform and said, "Oh, you three, I should have known. That is your father's setter, Maud. She showed up on the hill yesterday. She and that big dog of Jehann's spent most of the day sniffing the whole hill over. She barked a few times last night to come in. We ignored them, but they will not go away. We tried throwing pebbles and even yelling and they will not go. Do you three have any ideas?"

"How did Runty get here?" I said. "We took her to my uncle Wulfric's farm miles away at Quatford a month ago. Are you sure it is her?"

"Of course, I am sure. I can tell one dog from another."

I stood up. I could feel my legs fidgeting at the thought of petting her and running with her up and down the hillside and through the trees. Runty and Sir Jehann's dog, Big Boy, were hunting dogs who worked every day so I was not allowed to make a real pet of Runty, but I had become fond of her. And now she was back.

But the gates were closed and were to stay that way, Father would probably declare even though it was his dog outside.

How to get the dogs to go back to the farm? I thought. *For they must go back there. Uncle Wulfric can give them exercise and food which they cannot get here.*

I sat back down and asked Aethel if she had any ideas. She said no. Then I asked Rowena; she shook her head. I sighed. I had no idea. I could get Runty to come, but not to go.

"The only thing that Big Boy dislikes is the milk cow. And she has been slaughtered," said Aethel.

Aethel chewed on her upper lip. "Bert," she yelled up to her brother, "Big Boy is frightened of the milk cow, ever since she kicked him. He even avoids the smell of the cow. How about throwing cow dung at him?"

Bert started laughing at her. Then he told Manfred what she had said. Manfred started laughing too.

Godwin trudged past us, carrying rocks to the base of the tower for throwing later. Godwin went up the ladder to see what was so funny. He did not laugh at Aethel's idea, perhaps because his grief dampened his humor, or perhaps because he could see that it could be done. He told

Bert to go collect some dried pieces of dung.

Bert returned, not laughing any more. Manfred and Godwin had the sling poles in place. They tossed about a half dozen at the dogs. Big Boy yelped. Godwin called out that one piece hit Big Boy squarely in the side. Runty's bark grew fainter.

I worried, *Will they go back to the farm? Will they be willing to come back here after the Earl made the King's army go away? Will they now fear us?*

The dogs did not return that day. Word that Aethel's idea had worked was the story of the day. In fact at the end of supper, Sir Jehann stood up and told the whole story of the dogs arriving, staying, sniffing, marking territory, and leaving. He had not been there, but he told it as if he had been up on the tower judging it a good idea and sending Bert. Then he described the dogs leaving as if he had seen it.

Aethel was smiling, clearly pleased to have been of some help. I was pleased that the dogs were not harmed, but wished that it had been my idea. However, Aethel smiled such a big, honest smile as Sir Jehann told the story that I had trouble feeling out of sorts.

I decided to go see if I could make a useful suggestion too. I went up to Father and sat on the bench beside him.

"Maud, my dear, what brings you up here?"

"Father," I started nervously. "I was thinking. Could we not tie a note to the leg of a bird, like a jay? I heard one outside today. It could take the note to the Earl and ask him to hurry here."

I could see Sir Jehann try to hide a smile behind his hairy hand. Father was trying to stifle a smile. I thought, *Well, they laughed at Aethel's idea too. But then they tried it and knew that her idea worked.*

"Ah," Father was still trying to remain serious. "If one could train a Jay to fly with something on its leg, fly one place in particular, know where the Earl is so the Jay could be taught to go there, train the Earl how to read, and keep the Jay here while you did all that training, it might work."

I thought, *It is no use. My ideas are nowhere near as good as Aethel's.*

DAY 21, WEDNESDAY

I brought in five onions from the dew-wet garden to the sound of stones hitting the castle wall. I felt like Runty the dog and wished I could run off. I wondered where she had gone.

Aethel and Rowena were right behind me with their baskets of weeds. I delivered the onions to Mildred, while Aethel and Rowena handed the baskets to Mother. I wiped my hands on my dress, trying to get the dirt off without water.

I wandered over to Mother's side as she sorted. Only a few of the barely grown weeds went in the edible pile, most went back in the baskets for the horses. Mother handed a basket to Rowena. Rowena gave me a look that seemed to say what-did-you-do-to-get-out-of-this-chore and went to deliver them.

I continued to stand beside Mother. She gazed at me with warm, brown eyes. She put an arm around my shoulders. She asked, "My little Maud, are you feeling well?"

"I need a hug."

She gave my shoulders a squeeze.

"And I have a question."

A smile appeared on her face. "When do you not

162

have a question? What is this question?"

I had come up with a plan the night before as I lay on my mattress. Perhaps she would approve and take the idea to father. "Why can we not use a rope ladder to let one of the men over the wall to go hunting or fishing?"

She looked out the open window before answering. She was considering my idea. "Hmm, I am not certain that I have heard that proposed before. Though I guess your father would fear for the life of the one to go. He has told me that the army has men watching us from all along the foot of the hill to make sure we do not leave and others do not join us. Still, you may want to ask him."

I did not go run to ask him. *I know,* I thought, *Father will have no more respect for my idea than he did last night. I will need time to think how to say it differently to him.*

After another shorter pause she asked, "Is your question from hunger, my dear?"

"Yes. I am hungry all day long. And from boredom. I want to have food and I want to be free to go outside."

She seemed shocked. "Did you think your father would let you be the one to go over the wall?"

"No. Well, yes. But not really." I took a half-step away.

"Ah Maud, your father will never allow you to be in danger like that. Hmm. How to get through boredom? Mildred here says we must be more patient. I am not always patient myself, you know. We simply have to wait and keep telling ourselves this could be over tomorrow. You can hold on until tomorrow, can you not dear?"

I nodded. I was trying to hold back tears and so did not dare speak. I was busy trying to keep myself from yelling that I did not want a large idea like Patience. I was tired of being hungry and tired of being bored and tired of being stuck inside these castle walls. I was frightened in here too. More frightened in here than I would be running to Shrewsbury. I could feel tears forming, but I knew that Mother called yelling with tears a baby tantrum.

So I left the kitchen and walked slowly over to the little altar. No one was here. People could see me, but they would let me be alone. I had seen that no one bothered Father Cuthbert when he was over here kneeling.

I started crying. My eyes were probably turning red, and my nose was definitely running. I startled when Aethel put a hand on my shoulder.

"I did not mean to scare you," she said. "Rowena is in the kitchen, sitting there, doing nothing, so I came to be with you."

"Can you go away? I am not in a good mood for

play, or anything else."

Aethel sat down and put her arm around my back. When I looked over at her, I could see tears welling up in her eyes too. *Is the sight of someone crying enough to make her sad too?* I thought.

She asked me why I was crying.

"I am so very, very tired of being in here. I want to go out. The Earl's army is not here to rescue us. Father will not let us even risk the danger of seeing over the wall. And I cannot withstand it any more."

"Oh," whispered Aethel. "Me too. Grandmother lets me cry at night. She hugs me and tells me that we are all crying at night. Are you?"

"No. My parents might hear me," I said.

"Too bad. Grandmother says everyone is scared and tired of all this. She says the men are less scared because Father Cuthbert hears their confessions and gives them advice. But she says Bert says that Father Cuthbert's advice is not always very comforting and sometimes Bert is even more scared after confession than he was before it."

I forgot myself for a moment and asked, "What kind of advice does he give them?"

"I heard great-uncle Wulfstan tell Grandmother that the priest told them to be willing to die as our Lord did. That sacrifice is part of our religion."

My eyebrows moved up my forehead. "Is it?"

Aethel shrugged. "Anyhow, your father must have told Father Cuthbert to stop that because he has not said that again to great-uncle."

I was feeling better now. The tears had stopped. "Thank you, Aethel."

"You can come over to our mattress if you want to cry at night," she offered.

We hugged each other and walked over to the cherry tree where we could sit quietly until my face was no longer red.

***

After sitting there a long time, I reached up and grabbed a wild cherry blossom from the tree. I smelled it and held it delicately. These were at the white and fragile stage. After a bit, I began to pluck the petals.

"Aethel," I asked, "do you still want to go inside the great hall and hear what the men talk about?"

Aethel looked at me with a puzzled face. "When did I say that?"

"Oh, some days ago, I guess," I said, plucking more petals.

"You really do remember things people say. I do

not remember saying that, though if you say I did then I must have." She paused and then continued, "No, I do not want to listen to them. Their talking will be as boring as the women in the kitchen, but they will go on about different...oh, what is that word?"

"You mean in different ways?"

"No. But that word will do," she said.

Aethel stopped talking when she saw her great-uncle Wulfstan come out of the hall. He looked angry. He walked along the wall of the hall towards us until he came to the corner where he sat down, obviously wanting to be alone. He sat down on the dirt with his back to the rough oak post.

Bert came out soon after and looked around. Then he walked over to Wulfstan and sat down beside him, less than ten feet away.

"Uncle, are you all right?" Bert asked.

Wulfstan shifted to look at Bert so I could no longer see his face from where I was sitting.

"I will be," said Wulfstan in a still angry tone. "Give me some time to cool down. What helps anger is fishing for a few hours. A sure cure."

That is very true, I thought.

He looked at the ground by his feet. Bert saw us; I thought he might say something sassy but he ignored us.

Aethel and I whispered to each other, trying to work out what was making Wulfstan mad.

"That Jehann," said Wulfstan, "knows how to provoke a man."

They sat there quietly.

Then Wulfstan spoke again, "Should not let it bother me. I am proud to be a Saxon. We are not less men than those Normans. You should be proud too, my boy."

"I am, Uncle, I am. I would far rather be a Saxon than Norman or Welsh. I would not stop being Saxon even if they made me king."

"Yes, Normans been ruling us since I was a young lad. About your age I was when I first laid eyes on a Norman. Young knight with his mustache and beard all shaven off and no braid. That short haircut those Normans like. I never seen anyone like him. Then at seventeen I swore allegiance to Earl Roger, Earl Robert's father, and I been a man-at-arms for them ever since. See, it is the number of years that I served faithfully and well that make me think I ought to have more respect from Jehann. So when he is like he was in there, I..."

"Jehann is always Jehann," Bert replied. "We can do nothing about that. You yourself told me that when I was angry at him for giving me no credit for catching all those stray cows last October."

"Yes," Wulfstan admitted, "I remember saying that. And would not feel so strongly now if we could get out and go fishing and be apart from each other. It is the being in the hall or stable or tower all day long that is making us all feel so strongly, you know, but here we are stuck. A great Norman siege."

Wulfstan feels exactly what I feel, I thought. *I want to go fishing and walk through the woods. Does he want to make this end today too? I must try to ask him later if he has any plan.*

Curiosity finally made Aethel go over by her great-uncle. She knelt down on the ground on this side of him.

"What happened?" she asked.

Wulfstan looked her in the eyes, no longer so angry.

"Well, my girl, Sir Jehann was in there talking French to William and Chrestian. I asked him what he was saying because I understood enough of the words to know he was telling them when to be on watch. So Jehann says that he is asking them when they want to be on watch the next few days. For they are our professional men-at-arms, the Earl's best he says and they should have first choice to what suits them."

He continued, "I let that anger me. Now I am

better for talking with my nephew and niece." He gave Aethel a hug. "I will go back in and take the watch those young Norman pups do not want."

He and Bert stood up and went back to the hall. Aethel jumped up and ran back to me. Once her brother and great-uncle were out of earshot, Aethel asked me if I had heard all that.

I nodded. I thought, *This does not make sense. Will Wulfstan make trouble if he is still stuck inside these walls tomorrow? What will he do when the Earl arrives and praises his Norman men-at-arms?*

"Do you think Jehann meant to offend great-uncle Wulfstan? I do," she said.

"No, I doubt it," I said. "You know how Jehann can say things without looking to see whether it hurts you."

"Maybe," she said, "but you must admit Jehann thinks less of Wulfstan than William."

"I suppose he does. I know my father thinks well of Wulfstan," I said, trying to make her feel better.

"Yes, your father is not as proud as Jehann. He is more like a Saxon."

"What is that supposed to mean?" I could feel my face warming.

Aethel drew back at my angry face. Then we

heard Ulrica yell our names from the kitchen doorway. Aethel said sorry. I wanted to forgive her, but not right away. I thought, *Going fishing with Wulfstan would cure it all, but we can not have that until the Earl arrives.*

DAY 22, ASCENSION DAY

Heavy fog descended during the night. I could hardly see to the castle gates that morning. I thought, *That means the river valley below must be even foggier. The King's army must also be unable to see in the fog. Will Earl Robert use the fog to hide his army?*

The fog did not lift as the morning went on. Mother said we could go outside if we listened for the horn, so Aethel and I decided to take a walk around the castle yard.

We walked single file through the row of half-grown carrots in the vegetable garden over to the castle wall. I thought, *I can not believe that I have so little to do. I am walking for no reason but to get outside and have no destination. Perhaps if we see Wulfstan I could casually ask him if he had a plan.*

We walked carefully on the grasses growing along the wall. As we came to the end of the garden, we walked over the patch of ferns behind the wild cherry tree. The branches of the tree were low enough that I had to duck my head down as low as my shoulders as I went under them. I was careful to avoid stepping on the nest of lapwings in the ferns.

We walked to the south behind the great hall, and then turned east to the stable. We walked right behind the privies. I held my breath as we went past them. I heard Aethel cough and stopped walking.

I asked her if she was well.

She caught up beside me. "I am fine," she said. "They stink, but not as bad as the manure pile over there." She pointed to the pile on the side of the stable. I thought, *How will the men get all that in a cart to take to the barley fields? Will they have to find another cart or take more than one trip? Probably one cart and definitely more than two trips.*

On the other side of the stable, the tied bales of hay were nearly gone. We walked over the cobblestones and the small grassy area where the horses grazed.

We turned north and changed course to pass in front of the smithy and the cow shed and the pig pen which were less than a foot from the wall. The smell of manure was no longer strong here. The animals had been dead too long.

On the other side of the pig pen, we could walk right next to the wall again until we came to the little altar. Luckily, the priest was not there and so I could walk right in front of it, close enough to touch the altar linens if I had wanted. I thought, *Will this altar be taken somewhere else once we can go to mass in the new church?*

From there we took a few steps north to the castle

gates. Aethel walked up to the gates and put her ears up to the crack between them. I joined her and listened for a few minutes. All I could hear was birds, willow warblers most likely. They usually nested in the willow trees.

I heard something moving. I thought, *Are there deer on the other side of this gate? Can they hear me? Can I slip outside in this fog? Can I slip out unseen? Is someone willing to help me?*

I was about to ask Aethel if she could think of a plan when Bert approached, rolling a wheelbarrow up the path.

Aethel asked him what he was doing. He stopped the barrow and put his finger on his lips, motioning us to be quiet. He pulled the barrow into the base of the tower and motioned for us to come closer.

"Me and Wulfstan heard a dog or man up on the hilltop," he whispered. "Cannot see him in the fog. I fetched some dry horse dung."

I was about to ask if it could be a stag or a doe he heard when he pointed to the great hall. "Maud," he said, "go quietly to the hall and get your father or Sir Jehann to come help us throw dung at the intruder. Aethel, help me load the bucket."

When I returned with Father, Aethel was handing a bucket up to her brother on the ladder. Father grabbed the sling poles and followed Bert up the ladder.

I really wanted to go up the ladder too. I thought, *But Father has not changed his mind. Somebody might be on the northern slope, waiting for another victim like Edric.* So Aethel and I stood there quietly, listening to them loading and tilting the sling poles. The men must have been gesturing and pointing because I could not hear them talking, even quietly.

Suddenly, I heard a man cry out from the other side of the wall. That man must have been what I heard moving by the gate. Bert came clambering down the ladder quickly and motioned for us to help him load the bucket with rocks.

"At least one man out there, so we switch to rocks," he whispered. "I should have liked to have seen that fellow's face when great-uncle Wulfstan pelted him." He chuckled quietly.

With a load of rocks, he quickly climbed back up the ladder. Again, I listened. The weight of the rocks in the sling poles made a swooshing sound as the rock went flying. I heard no more yells. Though I did hear Father say "Hit one."

Bert came back down for another bucketful of rocks. Aethel and I helped him load it, and he headed up the ladder again. The slinging of the rocks went on and on.

Only once more did we hear someone over the wall cry out.

"I am going to try to get up there now that the firing has stopped. Stay here with me until the fog lifts and I can find a chance," I whispered.

When the fog finally started to thin, Bert came back down the ladder with the sling poles. He told us, "Go inside the kitchen. No one to fire at here, and they over there will throw stones."

Aethel told him he was not our boss. Then he asked if she wanted to repeat that to Grandmother. I told him I needed to talk to Father up there, but he shook his head and pointed to the kitchen.

***

Later, Wulfstan came into the kitchen. He walked over to his sister Mildred who was frying meat in a large cast iron pan.

"Mildred," he said. "I only now came down off the watch tower and am parched. How about a mug of ale? I have had a long day."

Mildred nodded and motioned to Edwina to fetch a mug of ale from the cellar. Edwina nodded back and hurried off.

Wulfstan sat down on a stool beside the fire where

Mildred was cooking. He asked her if she had heard about the dung.

Mildred had heard the full tale from Aethel already, but shook her head because she could see he was in the mood to tell his tale. I moved closer to hear him better.

Wulfstan straightened his back like he does when he recites a story. He began, "Bert and I were on watch a little after breakfast when we heard rustling over in the bushes by the church, you know the ones I mean. Could tell it was larger than a hare or a small doe, but it might have been Peter's setter again or even a man. I did not want to harm that pretty little hunting dog of Peter's, so I told Bert to fetch some of the horse dung."

Edwina came back with his mug, and he paused to drink. I grabbed the edge of the work table and held on to keep from fidgeting so that he would not be distracted in his tale.

"Well, Maud here had fetched Peter. Bert and Peter and me started throwing dung in the sling poles. We were aiming at the bushes near the church. That fog made it hard to tell, but we aimed in that direction at any rate. Heard someone cry out. I think it was one of my shots."

He handed the mug back to Edwina and wiped the foam from the ale off his mustache and beard. He asked

Mildred if he could have more. Mildred shook her head and poured water in the mug for him.

Wulfstan frowned at her and continued, "Once we knew we had men up so close on the hill, we switched to rocks. Fired more than two score. And not only over by the church. I thought I heard them on the Hollybush road to the west so I started swatting them like the pests they are."

Mildred interrupted, "You hit any?"

"I think Peter did. We heard a groan."

"Do you think they did any damage out there?" she said. "I mean to the church?"

Wulfstan paused to drink the water. "Hmmm. Peter is wondering that too. We may need to throw some rocks into the camp over there. I cannot say more about that."

"Could it not have been the Earl's men on the hill?" Edwina asked.

"Girl!" he said. "Why would the Earl's men be sneaking around? All they have to do is say who they are and which Welsh prince sent them."

I was glad I had not asked that question.

Wulfstan stood up slowly. He looked very tired and full of aches. He set the mug down, thanked her, and left the kitchen.

I thought, *Maybe Father will need someone to go*

out there and look at the church and the camp. I am small and fast. Not as fast as Rowena, but certainly faster than old Wulfstan. I need to ask Father. But how to ask without failing?

After he left, Mildred assigned everyone tasks for preparing supper. Supper was to be stew with carrots and the meat she had browned. They also made barley bread with only a spoonful of wheat flour. I frowned. I prefer bread made from finely milled flour without lumpy barley.

DAY 23, FRIDAY

The lettuces were now leafy and green and of a good enough size to harvest. This morning Aethel and I harvested a few of them at the end of the row near the wall, while Rowena started at the end of the row near the walking path. Working silently, I bent down and picked leaves of lettuce carefully from the plant, trying to leave the roots and as much of the stalk as possible. I stopped for a moment when I spied Godwin.

"Rowena, look," I called over, "your father has come down from the watch tower."

Rowena did not look up from the lettuces. "Maud, cut it out! I know you are tempting me to look there and I will not."

"I was not…never mind."

I was so stunned by Rowena's anger that I had trouble focusing on the lettuce head. I thought, *Why is she upset by the sight of the tower? She was not like this the last time we weeded. Or was she?*

When I finished with a lettuce head, I placed the leaves carefully in my basket at the end of the row.

After my next trip to the basket, I did my best to keep my attention on the lettuces and not a small blue butterfly, about the size of a large moth, which had landed on a carrot top near me. I stared for a moment and then looked back at the lettuce. A few plants later I found myself staring at the castle wall which was now only a few feet away. It was so thick, so solid. I sighed.

Aethel looked up from her head of lettuce when she noticed me stop pulling.

"Are you daydreaming again?" Aethel asked.

I stood up and pointed at the wall. "No, not really. I was wishing for a hole in this wall. If a goddess or someone like that walked over here right now, I would wish for a single window so that we could see the army and see the hillside and the trees."

"Are you crazy? A window would let the army see us and maybe even attack us through it," she said.

"That is precisely why I was sighing. I know that I cannot have a window, but I still wish for one."

"Huh?" Aethel asked.

I sighed and squatted down again. She was plainly unable to understand, so I tried to keep my mind on the garden. If I made a mistake someone would go without food. We harvested eight heads of lettuce, enough for salads at supper.

When I gave the lettuce to Mildred, she said, "Go ask your father if you can play outside now. I heard the song birds singing a rain song. Most likely will rain after mid-day."

I wandered over to Father at the base of the tower as casually as I could and waited politely for him.

"Maud," he said. "How is your day going?"

I knew I was told to ask about playing, but decided to try another topic. "Boring. I helped to pick lettuces and now there are no chores. I was wondering…Do you want someone small and quick to help you?" I could feel my chest tighten as I asked.

"Help me?"

"Yes, I heard that yesterday you were wondering how much damage might have been done to the new church. And I have this good idea. I could climb up on the wall and lower down on a rope with knots in it every foot on the east wall and I could-"

He interrupted with a laugh. A gentle laugh, but it hurt like a harsh one.

He stopped laughing. "Oh, my child, you do have a big imagination. Do you not remember what I told you about sieges this spring? Remember that day you and I took the dogs to your uncle's farm? I said in a siege no one leaves. No one. We wait. Earl Robert will be here tomorrow. You must believe that. Think how silly you will feel when he arrives and you doubted him."

I nodded to show I had heard. I wondered, *Does*

he really believe the Earl is nearly here?

"May I," I said, my voice barely under control. "May I help some other way?"

He looked around the castle yard. "No, no other errands. Squires and servants are felling trees to the north. We will shoot at them. They will shoot at us. You will be safe in the kitchen."

I sighed, "Yes, father."

He nodded, and I went to the kitchen where I found Aethel talking to Ulrica. I did not tell her about asking my father. I hated how I had failed.

***

That night at supper we had beef pie and large salads with spiced oil dressing. The pie had too much onion and too little meat for my taste, but I knew better than to complain. Mother and Mildred were doing their best.

"I heard," said Aethel, "Manfred and my brother. Manfred says he was on watch and saw some of the trees made into logs and loaded on wagons and delivered to the army camp. The other trees were made into lumber right there along the Oldbury road. Bert asked him if they were building something and Manfred said 'Not Yet'. What do you think they will build? A hall for the knights? A bath house?"

"Perhaps they will make a bridge between the two hills," I said.

Rowena said she had no idea and pecked at her food. She did not seem very enthused by the trees, wagons or supper.

I walked up to Father and asked him how shooting at the King's men had gone.

He put his arm around my waist. "We shot many bolts and arrows," he said. "We also fired rocks from the sling poles. I think Manfred hit one and Sir Jehann hit four. We certainly kept them from cutting trees close to this castle. They had to stay back by the Oldbury road. You will probably be in the kitchens again tomorrow, as we try to keep them from working again."

He pulled me into his lap and I stayed there.

At the end of supper, Wulfstan stood up and sang one of his favorite songs, "Lusty in the Merry Month of May." Wulfstan always sang the verses to it, and everyone else sang the chorus. We all knew the words to the chorus, and many older people mouthed along during the verses. I liked the chorus.

> Lusty in the merry month of May
> Orchards of wild cherry trees in bloom
> Gusty winds will blow the blooms away

One kiss and I will be her bridegroom

Once the song was over, we all asked Wulfstan to sing some more. He agreed and sang a summer song about hay harvest and another about evening sun. It passed the time until the mattresses were to be brought out.

DAY 24, SATURDAY

For breakfast, we had some fried strips of beef that were cooked like bacon, as well as porridge. The porridge was thicker than usual this morning though without cream on it.

I leaned over to Rowena. "Why are we getting more food today?"

She shrugged. She had taken very little porridge and had eaten only half of it. "He would have liked meat for breakfast," she said.

I nodded. Then I rose and went over to ask Mildred at the next table.

"Yes," she said, "good to eat your fill this morning, hmm? The men need to eat their fill because they will work hard today. Bert, Wulfstan, Manfred and Godwin will be chopping down the Maple tree. Sir Jehann, Peter, Chrestian and William will be standing two watches each to make up for the lumber jacks. A hard day of work."

As she spoke, she moved her whole portion of beef onto Bert's plate. He scowled and when she was done speaking he told her, "Grandmother, you will work today too. You take it."

She smiled at him and said she had already had

186

plenty of porridge. I doubted that. I had seen her pour almost half of her porridge into Aethel's bowl a few minutes earlier. I said nothing. I knew to contradict her could earn me a slap on the hand.

***

Rowena, Aethel, and I quickly finished our chores of clearing the breakfast tables, weeding the garden and bringing in more heads of lettuce. The thought of arrows flying scared me and I barely paused to daydream or notice the birds singing. Though Rowena worked a slow pace. When we finished, the three of us headed for the Maple tree.

I would miss the tree, and I felt sad that the budding leaves on it would never turn yellow. I knew my chance to climb again was gone. But I also felt a thrill of having something to watch, something new to break the boredom.

When we arrived at the tree, we found most of the low hanging branches had been brought down with a pruning hook. We had also missed most of the standing around and discussing the task.

Rowena walked up to her father. "Father, what will happen to the birds that were nesting in the tree?"

Godwin smiled at her and answered, "You missed

seeing Bert climb all the way up the tree trunk this morning to fetch down the nests. One of them was old and abandoned. The other two he set up in the cherry tree." He pointed over there. "I do not know if the birds will like their new home, but it will surely be better than staying in this log."

I ran over to the cherry tree. I wondered if the birds had inspected their moved nests yet. I could see the bottom and sides of the nests, but not what was in them. I could hear no chirping.

When I returned to the Maple tree, Manfred and Bert were throwing ropes over two of the large, mid-height branches. They anchored the ropes to the ground with long wooden stakes. Watching them, Wulfstan complained to Godwin, "This wood will be too green to burn properly for months. Why are we taking the tree down now? The siege is bound to be over before the logs age."

Godwin looked at Wulfstan as if he had already answered this at least once. "I know it will be green. Peter says to chop it, so we chop it. You and I both know there are ways to age wood quicker."

"Quicker yes, over night no." Wulfstan shook his head sadly and scratched his silver beard. He walked over to where the axes were resting against the stable wall. Godwin had sharpened three axes and a hatchet that morning.

Godwin walked up to the trunk and made four chalk marks at shoulder height on the exact points for north, east, south and west.

I nudged Rowena and whispered to her, "Ask him why we can not use the pig pen or cow shed walls for firewood."

Rowena nodded and then politely asked.

He looked at me and answered. I wondered if he had heard me say it first.

"So you want to know that. The stain and oils in the shed lumber will be very smelly as it burns. We are much better off using this good-smelling Maple wood. Do you understand that, little Maud?"

I nodded. Of course, I could understand that. I thought, *Why when I ask some questions do the adults act like I asked too simple a question and must be simple myself to not know the answer already? That one did not seem too simple to me.*

Wulfstan spotted us standing a few feet from Godwin and told us, "Go sit by the wall to the hall. The tree will not fall that way, hopefully."

I spotted Father Cuthbert standing against the wall and aimed myself for the corner of the wall furthest from him.

"I do not want to sit so close to the privies," said Aethel.

"I would rather smell the stink of the privies than be near the priest. He might pray for the tree and make us join in, or he might give us a sermon on how sin causes a great fall."

Aethel and Rowena agreed.

The men took turns chopping. When they started to look tired, Aethel and I brought water to them to drink. They all stopped and had a break.

Wulfstan grinned at Manfred and teased him, "So how will you get along without your tree to scratch your back on? Where will you act like a bear?"

Manfred laughed. Then he stretched his arms out like an animal in the sun. "Perhaps I will go without a back rub," he said. "Or perhaps I will get my wife to scratch my back. But, most likely I will go without."

The men all laughed and resumed chopping.

From where they were weakening it, the tree should have fallen directly in the center of the cobblestone area between the smithy and stable. After many, many chops, it came down a bit south of there. Some of the branches scraped the wooden slate roof and siding of the stable as it fell.

Manfred ran up to the stable and looked carefully

at the roof and walls. He then announced it was fine. Godwin and Wulfstan both stared at the trunk and frowned.

"I have felled many trees in my life, but rare had the tree as many obstacles to avoid as this one," said Wulfstan to no one in particular.

Godwin and Bert grabbed the two-man saw with handles at each end and began sawing the base of the trunk into pieces between one and two feet in length. As they finished the first piece, Rowena called out to her father and asked him how old the tree was.

Godwin crouched down and began counting the rings of the tree. He called out forty-two.

Rowena and I stared wide-eyed at each other. I thought, *Forty-two. That tree must be older than Godwin himself.*

Wulfstan grabbed the hatchet and began hacking off large branches. Manfred picked up the pruning hook and started taking small branches off of the large branches still on the trunk.

As he worked his way up the trunk, Wulfstan called out to Manfred and Godwin, "Do you think we can leave some of the trunk uncut?"

Manfred called back, "No. Peter said we had to make firewood of the whole thing."

"Pity," said Wulfstan, standing up. "This is fine Maple. Size of the trunk puts me in mind of a cubby stool that my grandfather made."

Manfred started to chuckle.

Wulfstan continued, "No, he called it a cubby stool, really. Anyhow, chopping it is a waste of good wood."

"Yes," said Manfred, "but Peter is not to be disobeyed on this."

"Mmm," said Wulfstan, "how about we save it for last and if he comes by I will ask?"

So they went to work on slicing the tree into a huge pile of thick disks.

"Why does your father want all the wood chopped?" Aethel asked me.

I shrugged and thought, *Why do we need so much firewood if the Earl is to arrive any day? Will we not then be free to take down trees on the hillside or by the river? Will there be more funeral pyres?*

As I watched the saw go back and forth and the sweat appear on the men's foreheads, an idea came to me. "Perhaps he wants to keep the men busy or give them exercise. Or perhaps he wants a huge pile of logs so it will look like we have enough wood that we are not in a hurry for the Earl to arrive."

"But we are in a hurry for that. And we all know it," said Rowena.

"Umm, oh, perhaps another reason," I said.

She rolled her eyes and turned back to watch the cutting.

The sawing and axing took the rest of the morning.

By mid-afternoon, Aethel and I were bored of sitting there watching, only getting up to fetch mugs of water. We decided to go see what was happening elsewhere. When we asked Rowena if she wanted to go, she said she was tired and wanted stay in the afternoon shade of the hall.

I led Aethel to the tower.

"Are you going to try to get up there again? I do not want to," she asked.

I could see my father's head and could hear Sir Jehann talking up on the tower platform.

"No," I said. "He will not give in."

I went to the bottom of the ladder. Sir Jehann had stopped speaking, so I called up for news. My father called down that a wagon of timber was being delivered to the army camp, but nothing else new.

For lack of anything else to do, we went back to the tree, where the men were now splitting the disks into logs. I did not see the base of the trunk among the disks.

"Rowena, where is the base of the trunk?" I asked.

She shrugged, but her face said she knew.

I kept looking around but could not see disks big enough to be the base. Perhaps it had been made into logs first.

"Maud, we should go to the kitchen. It must be time to help," suggested Aethel.

I nodded and we set off without Rowena.

When we arrived in the kitchen, Mother had us help put heaps of salted beef and salads on trays for supper. *If only we could dine this well for more than one day,* I thought. *If only the Earl would arrive, then we could go back to eating like this all the time.*

DAY 25, THE SEVENTH SUNDAY AFTER EASTER

During the Pater Noster in the Sabbath mass, the adults were all praying. So was Rowena. Usually, not everyone prays. Some say the words and have attentive looks on their faces, but most look around. This morning we all prayed. No one even looked up when two rogue clouds passed over head. I figured they must be hoping God will send the Earl this day.

Perhaps the Earl will return if we pray, I thought, so I joined in more loudly than ever before. Mother noticed me singing more loudly and stroked my hair.

***

Later that morning, we were sitting in the kitchen, confined there by rain and arrows.

"Will this rain bring a cool week?" I asked no one in particular.

Ulrica looked up from the bread dough she was kneading. She looked out the open door at the rain pouring down and said to me, "Well, it might, but this rain may not last that much longer."

Aethel stood up to look at the sky from the doorway. "Perhaps we will be able to go down to the river next week."

"I hope so," I said. "I feel like eating anything out there - strawberries, fish, venison, rabbit, river eels, elderberries. I think I am hungry enough to eat worms."

"Eww!" said Aethel with a look of disgust. Rowena lifted her head up to stare at me.

I grinned. "Well, maybe not. But there is so much good food out there."

Aethel grabbed her stomach. "Stop it. All this thinking about food is making me even hungrier."

Rowena opened her eyes again and broke in, "What are you complaining about? I saw your grandmother give you most of her porridge."

"Yes. She said she had enough." Her face grew serious, and she whispered, "I worry. She needs less food every day."

"She still needs the food," said Rowena. "She simply loves you more than her own need, right? Now you two leave me alone."

I heard Mother over by the oven tell Mildred, "The men bathed last night after working all day. I thought then that we could go without. I see the girls over there and I am changing my mind. What do you think?"

Mildred bustled over and told Aethel to stand. "You are filthy little lambs. Sabbath or no, you must be cleaned," she said.

Ulrica and I were sent to fetch buckets of water from the cistern. Luckily, the priest did not see us. We used a large clay bowl and washcloths as we had days before.

My skin felt so much smoother. I decided, *When this siege is over, I will try to bathe in the river every few days, all four seasons.*

***

Later, Manfred came in to the kitchen. Ulrica was sitting on a stool beside Edwina spinning wool on a drop spindle. He bent over Ulrica and spoke softly to her. I could not hear what he said or her reply.

After he left, I could hear Ulrica, Edwina and Mother, who had all heard him. "To be working like that on the Sabbath. Those men are very wicked," said Mother.

They all nodded in agreement.

"How big do you suppose it is?" asked Edwina.

"The hill is very round," replied Mother. "Very little flat ground over there for something like that to sit on. And what little ground there is, is covered by the tents, or at least that is what Peter says. So it must be rather small."

"Mildred, did you hear what Manfred said?" asked

Ulrica.

Mildred had been dozing on a stool up against the wall by the oven. "What? No, I did not hear him come in. What did he say?"

Ulrica smiled, happy to retell it. "Manfred says the King's men are building some sort of catapult over on the hill there."

I looked at Aethel with wide eyes. I asked Mother's permission to go play outside as the rain was almost stopped. Aethel asked her grandmother for permission.

"Maud," Mother chuckled. "Yes, you may go out. Do you think there is something new to see? If the men standing watch tell you to take cover, you come right back here."

I nodded and we ran to the watch tower. Bert and Wulfstan and Peter were standing under the timber doorway, very silent. Chrestian, William and Father Cuthbert were standing over in the garden by the wall, very quiet. So we stood there at the base of the tower, very quiet too.

I could faintly hear several hammers pounding. I wondered if the hammering was from the Oldbury road or the sheep pasture hill.

Aethel and I sat down on the dry brown dirt, inside

the base of the tower. The rain had not come in here. I was glad to be sitting. Standing made me tired. Father crouched down beside us.

"Maud, do you know what they are making?"

"Yes, Father. Manfred said it is a catapult."

He nodded. "Yes, but not a very large one. The base is about the size of the great hall door, and the lever is only about six feet long. They will build the machine over in the camp where they have smiths. They will bring the machine to the road on this hill when it is ready. Do not worry, my child. It will not be able to throw anything that could break through the wall."

"That is good, Father."

"Yes. The Earl and his Welsh princes should be here soon. Perhaps before it fires." He patted my back gently and shouted up for news.

Godwin's voice shouted down that it was the same as before.

"We had better enjoy being outside," I said. "Tomorrow we will probably be confined to the kitchen."

Aethel nodded.

When the clouds left, we lay down on the wet grass at the edge of the garden and closed our eyes to rest in the warm sun. Rowena came over and lay down too. Our nap only lasted a few minutes.

Mildred woke us. "Get up, you three, and gather the last eight heads of lettuce."

We were finishing in the garden, when several small stones made taps on the wall beside us. I looked up and ducked low at the same time as Aethel. Mildred called to us to hurry.

But I did not hurry. I thought, *Am I becoming accustomed to rocks being thrown at me? Will I bother to get out of the way if I see one coming at me?*
I watched a stone travel over the wall and land by the gate. My hands hurried of their own will. *No, I would never be able to ignore the rocks, not really.*

DAY 26, MONDAY

Aethel and I were pulling weeds in the vegetable garden again. This morning the sun was hidden behind a few fluffy clouds, giving us on and off light to find the weeds to pull. I thought, *We have been out here so often this summer that the ignorant weeds barely have time to show before being yanked from the soil. If I could go outside I would have so many more things to do and the weeds would have time to grow.*

I looked over at Aethel in the second row of turnips. She was bent down differently this morning. She was able to pull her legs closer; her legs were skinnier.

Rowena did not have to do chores. Mother had excused her from chores for the day when she fainted while carrying bowls of porridge in to the hall for breakfast. "Should I should try fainting for more naps?" Aethel asked.

I laughed. I heard the sound of a lapwing calling out. I thought the sad cry came from over in the cherry tree. I looked over there and tried to see the bird. The ferns on this side of the cherry tree were blocking my view.

A low rumbling noise traveled from beyond the wall. I stood, trying to hear it better. I yelled up to the watch tower, "What is that noise? Is it the Earl's army?"

Wulfstan's head appeared over the tower railing.

Heavy feet were thudding on the ground behind me. A quick glance told me that my question had drawn the men from the great hall.

Wulfstan yelled to them as well as me, "Good ears, Maud. Wagons coming up the cartway from the river near the bylet. King's men riding on horses and more horses pulling wagons."

Sir Jehann and Father were on their way to the tower, probably to survey the wagons. I thought, *What does this mean? Why is the army bringing wagons from the river?*

Wulfstan disappeared to the north side of the platform. Bert came down the ladder and started assembling the sling poles.

"Maud, we should finish the weeding before they send us inside," said Aethel from the turnip row.

I nodded and squatted down again. I smiled at the thought that I had helped alert Father to the wagons.

Father descended the ladder. He motioned to William who was now standing near Bert and the sling poles. Bert headed for Aethel. I moved closer to Aethel so I could hear his news.

"Little idiot," he said to her. "Go to the kitchen. More rocks today."

No news. Why, I thought, *does he have to call her that? Is he upset about William being picked to use the sling poles?*

I decided not to let him order me around. When Aethel scooped all her weeds into her basket, I went back to my row where the lettuces had been. I did not hurry. Our men were flinging rocks, but none were flying over the wall to us.

***

When I entered the kitchen, Father was there, talking to Mildred. I almost took a step back in surprise. I set my basket of weeds on the work table near Mother and listened.

"We must do it," he said. "We must give the Earl another day. I will not slaughter the mare if..." he paused. I could see he was almost on the edge of tears. "The chickens are not a necessity. They can be our supper tonight. If you have no milk cow, then we can not need the eggs for cake or...whatever."

Mildred took a moment to start an answer. "Peter, I know you love that mare. I also do not like that taste of horse meat. Yes, I tasted it once. Not very good. We do need the eggs from the chickens for your breakfast table and for thickening sauces."

Mildred's eyebrows arched from thinking hard. "I will take care of the chickens. You and Jehann must go without eggs at breakfast."

Father nodded, with a sigh that relaxed all the muscles in his face and shoulders. I had not realized how tense he was until he let go. He must have been very upset at the thought of losing the mare.

I thought, *Will the Earl arrive today? Will the bay mare be slaughtered tomorrow if he is still not here?*

He turned to go, and Mother stepped into his path. "Peter, may we work wool this afternoon? You and the other men will be outside."

He answered, "Yes, dear. The King's men are building that catapult base where the Shrewsbury road and Oldbury road meet. They are bringing in wagons of large rocks that were brought by boat. They dare not fire on us today for fear of hitting their own."

***

I was cleaning a fleece on the floor of the hall while the women spun thread and wove cloth that afternoon. My stomach was a tight knot in my belly. I could not stop thinking of food.

I watched the pile of carded wool in front of me grow, and my arms became tired. I thought, *How strange,*

I am hardly working, all I am doing is pulling the brush back and forth. How can this be enough tire me? Are the men out chopping trees along the road this tired? Probably not, they have plenty to do and plenty of food.

***

Mildred was cutting slices of roast chicken onto a serving plate in my arms, when I startled at a large thud. Mildred told me to set the plate down before I made a mess. Then Edwina, Aethel and I ran outside the kitchen to see what had caused the thud. I heard Aethel stifle a sob beside me. She was looking at the east wall.

I could see nothing different in the castle yard, no new rocks or arrows. However, I could spy Sir Jehann up on the tower platform. He grabbed the horn and gave it two blasts, which meant everyone was to stay inside. I decided to take a risk and run for the tower.

However, Mother had other ideas and grabbed my left arm and Aethel's right arm and dragged us all the way into the kitchen.

Nothing happened for several minutes. Then I heard another loud thud. This time it sounded like it had come from within the wall; the sound was similar to the sounds when the wall was being built, stone hitting stone.

"Mother, what is it?" I asked in concern.

She did not look at me, her gaze continued to look out into the yard. "Those *men* are trying out their catapult." Her voice was full of disgust.

Several minutes later, we heard a different sound. This one was more like the sound of an axe chopping into a tree. Mother made the sign of the cross and started praying the Pater Noster in Latin, so did Edwina. Then Ulrica and Mildred joined in.

I heard another thud out on the wall. I poked my head out and could see the wall was all there. No cracks. Mother scolded me and pulled me back into the kitchen.

Chrestian came limping into the kitchen. Ulrica grabbed the stool and helped him ease down on it. He pointed to me and waved me over. He spoke in French to me and told me to translate.

I nodded and he told me that he had been on the ladder. A rock hitting the wall shook the tower. He fell. His left leg hurt. I told all this to Ulrica.

She nodded and reached to pull off his left boot.

William appeared in the doorway but did not enter.

Mildred handed Edwina an enormous mug and told her to go fill it with ale.

Ulrica snapped her fingers to draw my attention. "Ask him if it hurts when I do this?" She lifted his foot off the ground.

He answered, "A little," before I could remember the French word for hurt.

Ulrica moved the foot and leg in several directions. He gasped only a couple of times.

Edwina brought the mug to him and handed it to him slowly.

"I thank you," he said. "You are gentle."

Mildred made one of her disapproving clucking noises. I looked at her but could not see what she meant.

"You are lucky," Ulrica told Chrestian. "The leg did not break. The thick boot leather probably kept the ankle from twisting. You hurt the muscles at the ankle. I will put some ointment on it and then you rest it."

While she mixed the ointment, Chrestian gulped and gulped the ale. He handed what was left of it to his brother, still in the doorway.

William stepped in to set the mug on a work table. Once Ulrica was done applying the ointment, William offered his shoulder to Chrestian to help him limp back to the great hall.

Mildred called out, "Chicken is all served up."

Mother went to the door and yelled for Father.

I crept up beside her. He leaned over the railing of the tower.

"Peter! Supper is ready. May we carry it to the hall?"

He thought a moment. Then he and Jehann talked back and forth. He leaned over the railing again. "Yes. Take as few trips as possible. If I blow this horn, run for the nearest building."

Manfred and Godwin must have heard him, because they appeared at the kitchen door and asked to help. Mildred loaded the trays more heavily than usual. Between us all, we were able to carry the platters of chicken, barley bread, water and ale to the hall in one trip.

I headed for the children's table, but Aethel headed for the women's changing room. No one had noticed her leave, so I followed her.

She was sitting facing away from the door, up on a wooden chest with her knees tucked under her chin. I sat down beside her. Sobbing, she did not budge as I put my arm around her waist.

Mildred poked her head through the door, saw me consoling Aethel and nodded to me. I nodded back and she left.

"What is the matter?" I asked.

When the sobs slowed she said, "You do not understand. You were not born here."

"What does where I was born have to do with why

you are crying?"

She turned to face me, and I pulled my arm back.

"You see," she said. "I said you do not understand. I was born here, in this great hall at Bridgnorth. I have never been any farther than my aunt's farm over that hill."

"And I was born in Quatford," I said, "and the Earl moved us here two years ago. So?"

She sighed. "So, I was frightened by those thuds this afternoon. What if the King brings down the wall and razes this place and makes us be servants somewhere far away, like Stourbridge or Bewdley? And what if they call me by my full name?"

"Aethelritha? No one is going to call you that. The name is very long," I said.

I thought, *I have not thought of being sent away. Rowena is always saying that we will all be killed, but maybe Aethel is right and we will all be split up and sent to work on another noble's land. What will happen to all of us? What do I say to her? I do not know what will happen. But if I say something that scares her, Mother will be mad at me. Aethel is my cousin and I should comfort her. That is duty.*

"Father will get us through this. Really, he will," I said.

She nodded. She knew it was what I was obliged

to say.

"We should go eat," she said. "I am really hungry."

"When are you not?" I teased her.

***

At the end of supper, Sir Jehann stood at his place at head table and made an announcement. "They, the knights of King Henry, have used their catapult on this afternoon today. You all heard it, no doubt. But you did not see it. It is a large arm of wood taller than a short man on a sturdy base with a round crank that makes circles around and around. The catapult is loaded with a big stone and then the knights, ah the squires actually, release the arm and away it goes that big stone."

He was gesturing with his arms to show the catapult arm moving. But he was no good at showing its size, and I wished I could see the real one outside.

"The first few firings went to the bottom of this hill. So I did not blow the horn then. I could see they were making no danger to us in here. It took them nearly an hour to find how to target this castle. When after that hour of misfiring, they did connect to the wall with a stone, I blew the horn twice, which meant all the servants were to go inside. That stone did no lasting harm to the wall that we can see, as I expected. When the Earl arrives with a large Welsh army that will conquer the paltry army of the King Henry and this is over, we will need to examine the wall better from outside. But I see no damage from the tower."

He sees no damage? I thought. *Perhaps they need younger eyes like mine to detect damage.*

He continued, "They fired a second stone at the wall. The second stone also hit the wall without damage to the limestone or mortar that I could see. I walked the perimeter and surveyed it all completely. Peter, did you see any damage?" Jehann paused long enough for Father to shake his head.

Jehann cleared his throat. "The third stone that was hitting the tower must have damaged the catapult or perhaps the men firing it did not know what they were doing for it takes much training to aim, load and fire a catapult and so it is damaged. Because the carpenters, or men who I presume were carpenters by their work and tools, could be seen working on it, seen by my own eyes.

"I truly believe, from my years of experience building and using catapults in sieges like this and even bigger sieges in Normandy at places none of you have visited that the catapult will not fire again this day or perhaps not even tomorrow. Though they have used local wood, so perhaps they can cut fresh lumber from fresh trees and shape it quickly, well as quick as wood shaping that they do goes. I shall have to see. Thus, I say to you all that tonight we should see no stones from the catapult, and tomorrow also, perhaps."

I thought, *Did God hear our prayers? Is that why the catapult was damaged? Perhaps the Earl will send the army to help before the catapult can be repaired. Perhaps I can go meet the Earl and hurry him on.*

DAY 27, TUESDAY

At breakfast, Rowena gave me almost all of her porridge. I shook my head no, but she got up and went over by the fireplace before I could shove the bowl back.

She helped Aethel and me clear away the bowls, but then she asked Mother if she could be excused from chores that day because she still did not feel well. Mother nodded quickly. I thought, *Why is Rowena getting out of chores so easily?*

Aethel and I weeded the garden alone. As we were starting in the carrot row, William and Chrestian were carrying lumber over to the base of the tower. By the time I finished in the garden and walked to the tower, their work was nearly finished. Chrestian was sawing the end off a small plank. I asked him what he was doing.

He looked at me and Aethel, who had tagged along, and laughed in a not very kind way. "I am sawing a plank. The last one. So busy were you with the garden that you have missed this project in whole."

"What all," I asked, "did you fix?"

"The floor was cracked by a large stone yesterday. You have heard of the new catapult the men of the King has, yes? Good, they landed two stones outside the wall. One of those broke and flew up here on the tower. You heard the one that hit the wall?"

We looked at each other. I knew everything he said already, but nodded respectfully to him in hopes he might tell us some new thing.

"Where did you get the wood?" Aethel asked.

"From the pig pen. No pigs. No pen needed, yes?"

"Oh, why do you need so much?" I asked.

He was now done. He carried the plank over to the ladder where he handed it to his older brother William at the top of the ladder. We followed him into the base of the tower, but he did not answer.

William teased him in French for being a lady's man and having so many female admirers. I frowned. Aethel asked me what they were saying and I translated it as best I could.

"I do not think," I said, "we should stay around those two if they are going to talk about us like that. We only wanted to know what was going on."

Aethel nodded, and we parted ways. I went to the stable, and she headed for the kitchen.

***

I was sitting on the bench in the stable beside Father, cleaning grass off a saddle blanket while Manfred put the reins on the colt so that he could be walked for exercise. Father had a sad look on his face. I wondered, *Is it because he misses his mare that was slaughtered this morning? Or is it worry about the siege?*

While Manfred worked, he asked a serious question. "Peter, why did we not dig a little more room in the cellar this winter so that we could have hung more meat down there?"

Father nodded as if it had been a fair question and was worthy of an answer. "We did not have the time. Remember how many Welshmen it took to build the wall and how busy that kept us all. Remember exactly how many cart horses you had to care for. Once the wall was done and the frost left the ground, I had all the farms to visit and warn. We had to bring as much grain here as we could find. Finally, the Earl planned this siege to last only two weeks. We had plenty of meat and grain for that. We still have plenty of water."

"Aye, easy it is to see what to do once it is past, as my father always said."

Manfred led the colt out of the stable. I took the saddle blanket back to the pile of saddle tack beside the wall.

I summoned up the courage to ask him a question. "Father, will they bring down the wall with that catapult?"

"No, child. I do not think they can. The sheep

pasture hill is too curved to build a catapult large enough to bring down this fine wall. They know that. But they may be thinking that we do not know that and will be more frightened of that thing than we truly ought to be."

He stood and gave me a hug. Then he followed the colt and Manfred.

I wandered around outside the stable. The stable walls had no handholds, so I would need a ladder down here and up on the stable roof. I wondered how to lift one up there and keep it stable, if I was to climb up there alone. Manfred broke into my thoughts and asked me what I was doing.

To avoid telling him my plan, I decided to go look for Aethel, who was sitting in front of the kitchen.

"Aethel, what are you doing?"

"Watching my great-uncle up on the tower. He is standing watch now. William is done for the day."

Wulfstan was up there, with his hand cupped over his eyes to stop the sun's glare. He moved up and down the platform, his eyes scanning all around. Bert was leaning against the west wall, watching the army camp intently. I could tell that Wulfstan was finding nothing to keep his attention. I thought, *Does that mean the army knights must all be in camp?*

Suddenly, Bert ran for the horn. He blew two

blasts.

Hopefully, Mildred and Mother were done butchering the mare.

Mother poked her head out of the kitchen and motioned furiously for us to hurry inside. As I passed over the threshold, I jumped at the sound of a large thud. Another stone from the catapult had hit the wall.

My eyes scanned the wall for cracks from the kitchen doorway, until I heard the second thud, louder than the first one.

Mildred motioned for us to come over by her. She was pouring hot juices over something in the oven. As I came close I realized it was roast horse for supper. Aethel, needing comfort, put her arms around her grandmother's waist. I stood against the wall and tried to keep from jumping at each heavy thud. I tried to think of a ladder for the stable roof, but the thuds told me that I would spend this day indoors.

DAY 28, WEDNESDAY

No song birds or chickens were making noise this morning. Mother was the second one awake. We dressed together and walked to the kitchen. Mildred was already there lighting a fire.

I sat on the floor and listened to them plan the day's cooking. Mother tried to get Mildred to sit down and rest while they planned, but Mildred would have none of it. She set a pot of water on the fire and brought out the bowls and trays.

When breakfast was ready, I helped to carry bowls of porridge on a tray to the great hall. I was surprised to find the children's table about a foot closer to the head table. Rowena's mattress was still on the floor, and she was still on it.

I thought, *That lazy bag of bones has gone too far this time. She will have to get up when the food comes.*

I went back to the kitchen to get another load for my tray.

When I returned, Rowena was still asleep on the mattress. And no one was bothering her. Her uncle was not teasing her, her sister was not nagging her, and her father was not ordering her. I wondered why.

Judging by the look on her face, Aethel was

confused too. We sat down at the table, which had only two bowls and ate our thin porridge with no milk. I wondered if I was beginning to forget how fresh milk tasted.

I leaned over Rowena's mattress and asked her if she knew how to get a ladder that I could lift onto a roof.

Rowena grunted and mumbled something. But she stayed right there.

Then Mother and Edwina came over with a small portion of porridge. Edwina sat on the mattress they shared and put her sister's head in her lap. My mother tried to coax Rowena to eat. She gently put a cloth on her neck and chest and put the spoon up to her lips, trying to feed her like a baby.

I wondered, *Is Rowena ill? Or is she faking illness to get out of chores?*

Spoonful by spoonful, Mother fed her the bowl of porridge. She told Aethel and me to get busy clearing away the dishes.

As we walked side by side carrying trays back to the kitchen, Aethel whispered, "She was trying to get us out of there."

"What is happening to Rowena?" I asked.

"I do not know. Will they actually tell us?"

"Maybe," I said." Rowena will, if they do not. We

have to get back to the hall to ask her."

When we delivered the trays to the kitchen, Ulrica made us do Edwina's chore of washing the bowls and spoons, while Edwina stayed with Rowena. Then Ulrica handed us the knitting baskets.

Ulrica went to check on Rowena several times during the afternoon, but told me to stay in the kitchen. When I complained to Mildred that Rowena was my friend and so I had good reason to see her, she told me that Rowena had a fever and they did not want me or Aethel to have it too.

At supper, Mother sat on the mattress with Rowena, while Aethel and I ate at the table. She looked too tired to eat or talk.

DAY 29, THURSDAY

"Mother."

I found her in the late morning sitting by the door to the kitchen sorting spun wool. Sorting was not important. She was only trying to find something to do. Perhaps I had time to talk with her.

Her two brown braids lifted across her shoulders as she raised her head. "What dear?"

"Um, may I ask you about Rowena? How long is she going to lie in bed?" I was trying to keep my voice neutral.

"She, well... I do not know. Perhaps until after the siege ends. She has been growing so much this year. I think her body needed food more than most of us. So she is feeling it worse than you. She has not eaten her share of food since Edric passed away too. The grief of such a loss is bad at any time, but under these conditions I believe she will have a harder time grieving. Did you know that I lost a brother younger than me?"

I gave her a puzzled look. "Uncle Wulfric is older than you."

"Yes, I have an older brother, Wulfric, down at Quatford. But I also had a younger brother, Ulfwin. He was six years younger. I looked after him the way Rowena always looked after Edric. My little brother hit his head on a rock and drowned in the river while he and his friends were out swimming. I could barely talk for weeks. I could barely eat. I was miserable. Yet, I recovered better than Rowena will because I had no other pain in my life. Maud, be good to her and help her as best you can."

She smoothed the wool in her lap, probably trying to calm herself. I thought, *She is really worried about Rowena or the memory of her little brother is bothering her.*

I decided this problem of Rowena not eating needed thinking about with Aethel, so I thanked her politely and ran to the stables where I had last seen Aethel.

Aethel was sitting on a bench with Manfred, watching Bert brush the colt. Bert had taken the colt on a walk around the castle yard to get him some exercise. I motioned to Aethel and we left the stable. I led her over to the Maple tree stump where we could sit and talk more freely. I wanted to go walking for more privacy, but found I was too tired for that.

"What is the matter?" Aethel asked.

"Mother is really worried about Rowena. I think she wants us to help her."

"Does she have a sickness?" Aethel's forehead was puckered.

I knit my fingers in my lap, trying to keep from fidgeting. "She is starving. Mother says her body needs more food than you and me. She also does not eat all that she is given. We have both seen that. Anyhow, she needs to be persuaded to eat. Mother, I guess, will try to get her some more food."

"From where? Grandmother needs more food too. And so do I. I feel hungry all the time." Aethel clutched her belly, like she was remembering how hungry she was.

"We all do. I do not know how or where mother will get more food. We are to persuade her to eat. So how do we do that?"

Aethel shrugged. "You know her better than me, Maud. Before this siege she spent more time with you...and her brother."

Some ants were on the ground crawling between blades of grass. I watched them scattering, looking for food or whatever it was that they needed. I thought, *Aethel is right, I do know her better. How should I start talking to her?*

"Aethel, can you come with me? I have no idea what to say."

Aethel stood up. I took the warm hand she offered, and we walked to the hall. Several men were sitting at a table playing a game of dice. Father Cuthbert was kneeling beside Rowena's mattress. He was praying in Latin. I made the sign of the cross and sat down on the floor at the foot of her mattress. Aethel did the same.

When the priest finished the prayer, he stood up and spoke down to Rowena who was awake and looking up at him. "Child, you must not dwell on the death of your brother. He is now in the arms of God. You must go on. You must eat and see tomorrow. For the Church believes that you must not hasten your own death. Be a good child and eat your portion tonight. I will say prayers for you tonight as well."

Father Cuthbert, without waiting for a reply, walked over to the table where the men were sitting and watched the dice game. I figured he must be as bored as we all were. He must also care at least somewhat because he had tried to talk to Rowena.

"Well," I said, "that speech was bound to bore you to a nice nap."

Aethel and Rowena both chuckled.

"Thank you," said Rowena. "He was here a long time and I think he only left because you sat down."

"Glad to be of help," said Aethel.

"Is there anything I can do?" I asked.

Rowena shook her head and rolled over to face the wall. She drifted off to sleep after a few minutes. Then

Aethel whispered in my ear that she was going to the kitchen and that she would come fetch me when it was time to serve supper.

I stayed there until Rowena woke.

"You awake now, Rowena?"

"Yes. Did you stay here the whole time?"

"Yes," I said. "We have not had much time to talk like we used to do. Remember when we went out following rabbit tracks in the snow and were gone almost all day?"

"That was months ago," she mumbled.

"Yes, but we were alone in the woods and could talk and talk."

Rowena sighed. I decided I needed to be quiet and see if Rowena might talk next. I sat there running my fingers over my wooden cross, remembering the cold winter evenings when my father had whittled it for my sixth birthday. I thought, *Was that really six years ago?*

Rowena started to cry.

"Why do I always cry?" she said through her tears. "What is wrong with me? I keep thinking about him, the little rat. About how he was my chore, to watch him. I keep seeing him everywhere. He was such a pain, but I think about him more than I think about my mother. And she is gone too."

"I think a lot about the King's army," I replied. "And the river. And I think about your little brother. I want to go up on the tower and see the army and the world again."

"I feel so ashamed. I wanted to go up there so badly, and I was so jealous of him going up there."

I crawled over the mattress to Rowena's side and put my hand on her back. "I feel very guilty about being jealous of him too," I said. "But I am still curious about what the army camp looks like. Edric is gone and we might die too. I worry that the Earl's army might not arrive or that the King's army will fire something horrible in that catapult. I feel that if I could see the catapult then I might not be so worried. Is that wrong?"

"I feel like that all the time," she whispered. "But I thought you are always so...you always say your father knows all and that he says the Earl is coming soon so it must be."

"I do think my father is right, but I also want to know for myself. I want to see that army camp. May I not think both of those?"

She shrugged weakly. "I suppose so."

"I have so many questions. Why have you not been eating enough?"

"I mean to eat. I am hungry. But then I sit down at

our table and I think about Edric not being beside me, and I lose my appetite." An unwiped tear slid down the side of her nose.

"Oh." I looked over at the men. Manfred and Godwin had now risen from the table and were leaving. It must be their turn at standing watch.

"Rowena," I looked at her with hope, "can you not go sit with your sister during meals?"

She sighed exasperatedly, "You know that I may not sit at an adult table until next year. And being near Edwina is not going to cheer me, right?"

"You rest now, Rowena," I said. I knew why she was refusing food and was sure to find a way to help her eat.

"Right," she agreed.

***

That night at supper, I dished Rowena's slice of meat and salad onto a plate, along with my own. Joining Rowena on the mattress, I tried to imitate Mother and feed her.

Rowena resisted because she was older than me and felt she should not be mothered by someone younger. But I told her, "You are my friend. You would do this for me. Eat."

Rowena frowned, but agreed and ate a couple pieces of lettuce and about half her slice of roast meat. She said she was full. *Certainly,* I thought, she *has eaten more today than she did yesterday.* So I ate the other half of the meat and then my own portion.

Aethel had half of her grandmother's salad as well as her own. I took comfort that Aethel was not starving like Rowena. My stomach tightened. She was far too weak to help make a plan.

DAY 30, FRIDAY

After a breakfast of thin, watery porridge I was still hungry. I suggested to Aethel that we sit outside so we would not hunger by looking at the pots in the kitchen. We sat against the kitchen wall to watch the men come and go from the tower. Chrestian was up on the watch tower, holding the horn. He blew one long note.

The men in the hall all came running out towards the tower. Godwin came running from the smithy. When they were standing at the base of the tower, Chrestian called down, "Look out!"

Sir Jehann ordered Wulfstan and Bert to help with carrying stones. Then Jehann climbed the ladder up the tower to join Chrestian and William. Manfred and Godwin talked for a moment and then headed back to the stable.

Father walked past us and told us to get inside the kitchen.

I asked him why.

"They fire at us, and we will aim to hit the men on the catapult," he said.

I let out a deep breath, relieved that he told me the truth of it.

I stood in the doorway to the kitchen, only inside enough to be obeying Father, but outside enough to see what was going on. Aethel, Ulrica and Edwina stood behind me. A batch of stones came over the wall all at once. Some stones were as large as heads of cabbage; other stones were as small as apples. They landed all over the castle yard.

Bert darted out of the tower base and grabbed a rock as big as his own fist. It was completely covered in vellum paper and rope. The rope was trying to hold the stiff vellum paper to the odd-shaped rock. Bert held it up and examined it. It looked to me as if someone had worked a long time trying to make the ropes hold the bulky paper into that strange shape. Then he called up to the tower to see if more rocks were being loaded in the catapult. The answer was no, so Bert took his time walking back to the tower.

Sir Jehann had climbed down the ladder by the time he got to where Wulfstan and Father were waiting. I could barely see them in the shadow-filled tower base. Father was unwrapping the paper slowly. Then Jehann and Father walked into the castle yard where there was more light for reading.

I wanted to go see the note too, but I knew Father would not want me to risk being hit by a rock and would not want to read the note aloud to me. He could read and write well in French and a little in English. He could read better and faster than the Earl. I had heard the Earl joke once that "He did not need to read. He had servants to do that for him."

Sir Jehann could sound out words in French but that note would be hard for him to read. The note must be in French, I realized, because they did not ask Father Cuthbert to come join them. He could read only Latin and English.

Now I could see Father reading the note to Jehann. It did not take very long. I thought, *Is the note from one of the knights in the King's army, perhaps even from Lord Roger de Montgomery who is in charge?*

My knees were fidgeting. "Aethel, what do you think it says?"

"Hmm," she said. "Maybe the King's men are running out of rocks."

"Running out of rocks?"

Aethel nodded. "Maybe they have very few rocks left so they sent a note saying we need to stop throwing rocks at them."

We all laughed, even Mother and Mildred who were now standing behind Edwina.

"How can you joke about this?" I said.

"We cannot know from here, so why not invent an answer?" she said.

Mother moved back into the kitchen, so I ducked back after her. She was trying to get Mildred to sit down on one of the stools. Mildred looked very pale and unsteady on her feet.

"Mother, do you need anything?" I asked.

"No, Maud. What is all the commotion out there?" Mother said as she poured a mug of water for Mildred. She then had me tell the story of the rocks and the note while Mildred sat and drank the mug.

When I returned to the doorway, Father and Jehann had disappeared into the great hall. I wondered, *Are they reading the note and translating it for the Saxon men and Father Cuthbert?*

I decided to go pay a visit to Rowena who was sleeping in the hall. Someone needed to tell Rowena about all this. I ran fast across the castle yard, my heart pounding. When I entered the hall, everyone looked at me. Godwin and Manfred were here already. Father stood up as if to intercept me, but then sat back down on a bench again when I walked quickly to Rowena's mattress.

Rowena was awake and listening to the men.

"Your father finished reading the note."

I felt so angry at myself for missing the reading that I tried to kick my backside. All I succeeded at was bruising my thigh.

"What did it say?"

"I had trouble staying awake. I think it was about the Earl in Shrewsbury."

"Oh. That is all you heard?

"Sorry," she mumbled.

I took her hand in mine. "I really did want to see you, too."

We sat there quietly as the men filed back out of the hall. Even Father Cuthbert left. Now we had the hall to ourselves. I sat quietly, listening to Rowena's breathing as she drifted in and out of sleep.

"Maud," she said, awake again. "Why do you think things happen?"

"I suppose God makes them happen. Why?"

"I hope God had a reason for Edric dying." I could see a tear on her cheek. "I worry more about Edric being in Heaven than I do about us making it through this siege alive. At least I do today."

"Really? I trust that my father and the Earl will get us through this safely," I said.

Rowena wiped away the tear, which had traveled down her neck. "That was not your sincere voice, Maud."

"Actually," I stumbled. "I am starting to be worried."

"Are you? Welcome to what the rest of us have

felt since the Earl left or even before that."

"I am not a pessimist like you and your father. I still trust these walls and my father and the Earl."

"These walls did not save Edric."

I muttered no and gazed at my hands, useless in my lap. I thought, *Why have I not been able to look out or get out yet? Why am I content to wait like my parents tell me? Is it fear? I have not made a plan this morning. Will Rowena come up with a good plan today? The plan must have a way to keep everyone away while I get over the wall. I will stay here while she naps and then ask her.*

I heard Father yelling. I rose from Rowena's mattress and ran out of the hall, trying to locate him by his angry voice.

He was in the smithy, yelling louder than he had in a long time.

I stopped behind Ulrica who was at the front of the crowd which had gathered.

Godwin, also in the smithy, yelled, "What does it matter?"

I moved to see around Ulrica's left arm. Father and Godwin were standing almost at the rear of the smithy. Everyone else was out here on the cobblestones. Sir Jehann and Wulfstan were poised at the door of the smithy, ready and waiting to go in.

Father yelled, "What does it matter? Did I not give you a direct order? When I tell you to do something, then by all that is holy I want it done!"

Godwin lowered his gaze, but not submissively, more like a bull about to charge.

I started to edge around Ulrica so that I could go stand by Father. Ulrica grabbed my arm and motioned that I should stay.

Godwin raised his head again. "Have we run out of wood?" he said. "No! Did we cut up the rest of that perfectly good shade tree? Yes! Did we make you enough logs for more funeral pyres? Yes! So we did what you told us, oh Seneschal."

"I told you to cut the whole tree and here is part of it uncut! What makes you think you did as you were told?" said Father.

My eyes widened. I thought, *This fight is over the base of the Maple tree. No wonder that Rowena did not tell me where it went. Had she seen her father being disobedient?*

Godwin did not answer and did not lower his gaze.

In a steely voice Father said, "Godwin, I have to punish you."

"How?" Godwin replied in an equally steely voice. "Do I lose more children? One dead and one deathly ill. Me penned up in here and almost crazy. How are you going to punish me? What have I not already lost? Has anyone here lost as much as me? Have you?"

"You disobeyed and must be punished," said Father.

Wulfstan stepped into the smithy. "Peter, please listen -"

Father kept his eyes on Godwin and interrupted Wulfstan, "No. This is between Godwin and me."

I was glad Ulrica had stopped me from trying to go in there.

"But Peter," Wulfstan tried again. "It was my idea to save the wood. I wanted -"

"I am not interested in whose stupid idea it was," Father interrupted him, now yelling again. "Nor am I interested in how many of you it took to carry that huge hunk of wood in here. Obviously, Godwin did not do this alone! But I gave the order to him and so he is the one who disobeyed. The trunk is in *his* smithy. Stay out of this!"

Silence was loud in my ears. Then I heard sobbing. Edwina was bent over Mildred's shoulder, crying. Mildred was rubbing her shoulder tenderly.

"Jehann, when does Godwin stand watch again?" he said.

Sir Jehann put his thumbs in his belt and

answered, "Tonight, or perhaps tomorrow, if you wish me to change the roster of the watch? I could - "

"Let him stand watch tonight," Father interrupted Jehann. "In the morning when he comes off watch, give him some food and have him come chop the entire thing by himself. No helpers."

"The two-man saw -" said Wulfstan.

"Wulfstan, did I ask you to speak?"

Wulfstan shook his head no.

Father took a deep breath. Then he said in a calmer voice, "I am aware the saw requires two men. You may help with sawing it. But Godwin does the axe work, understood?"

No one moved. I decided, *The punishment is not too hard. One hard day of work after a night's watch. Father could have had him whipped or beaten. Is Father not actually that mad? Or has Godwin already paid in other ways?*

I turned to ask Rowena and realized that she was still in the hall and had not seen all this. As soon as Father gestured that we could all leave, I ran to the hall.

"Maud," she said. "Tell me what that yelling was all about."

I told her about her father's part in the missing log and his punishment. Her face showed no surprise about the log in his smithy, but she did frown at the punishment.

"Edwina warned him the other night. He should have listened. Do you think Peter will make him do more?" she said.

"No," I said. I smoothed my wrinkled, dirty dress over my knees. "Rowena, can I ask you something?"

She nodded.

"We need to help end this. We need to get out of here, before we all start disobeying or going mad. Do you have a plan yet?" I said.

She frowned her thinking frown, not her displeasure frown. "I have been thinking as I lay here. But it all involves doing things that could get us shot with arrows or punished for disobedience. And punishment is on your father's mind today, right?"

I ignored that question. "Rowena, your plans are still better than mine."

"Yes," she conceded. "But I still could not act on them without you."

I gave her hand a squeeze and headed for the door where Aethel was waiting.

"Why did you not come over by me and Rowena?" I asked.

She shrugged.

I thought, *As much as I want to be free, it does not*

look likely today, if Rowena has no plan and Father is in a foul mood. I looked around the castle yard. "Pretend fishing in the pig pen?"

***

We had horse meat and onion soup for supper, with no bread. I ate at the children's table, while Edwina sat down on the mattress with Rowena, getting her to eat. I decided that if the soup had been thicker and had fish in it, then it would have been tasty.

After supper, Father stood up from his bench at the head table. He gestured for everyone to listen. I put down my mug and tried to sit as quietly as I could.

"As you know Lord Roger de Montgomery, the leader of the King's army over on the sheep pasture hill, sent a note today. It asked us to surrender. We will not surrender. The Earl is taking longer, far longer, than he expected. But he is waiting on the Welsh, so perhaps the delay is their …fault."

Several adults laughed. I thought, *Why is blaming faults on the Welsh always good for a laugh? Will they laugh when the Welshmen arrive with the Earl? Will they arrive? Should I try to go meet the Earl's army if he is trapped in Shrewsbury and not on his way here?*

Father waited until the polite laughter stopped and

then continued, "Sleep well tonight. Have faith that the Earl will be here very soon. Even if the Welsh do move slowly."

***

I was in bed that night listening to my parents putting the blanket on their mattress.

"Aedrica, grab that end of the blanket."

"You know best, dear," she replied.

"What?"

"Nothing. Never mind," she said.

They were quiet for the night after that. I wondered what she had meant.

DAY 31, SATURDAY

I woke up to the sound of my parents speaking on their mattress only a few inches from mine. I liked being able to hear them talking, which the others a few feet away could not.

"Aedrica, are you awake?" was the first thing I heard. Father's voice was whispering softly enough that I only heard it because my hungry stomach had me already awake.

"Now I am." Her voice was very sleepy.

"I do not think," Father sounded worried, "that Earl Robert is going to be able to lift this siege. Lord Roger de Montgomery's note over the wall yesterday said that the King had sent us this message that the Welsh Princes and the other Earls and barons refuse to support Earl Robert Belesme. That the Earl has surrendered at Shrewsbury. That the King will not harm the innocent inhabitants of this castle if we acknowledge his right to enter these walls. By which he means not harm the Saxon servants."

Mother rolled over to face him and interrupted him, "Peter, what in the name of the Holy Rood makes you think this note from King Henry speaks the truth?"

"Will you let me finish, woman?" He hissed and

then returned to whispering, "I can tell the King is speaking honestly because the banners of two Welsh Princes and William Pantoul are now camped out there with King Henry's own banner and that of Roger de Montgomery. He has their support. The Earl is not here, nor have I seen sight of any army in the distance. Nor I have seen the usual merchant boats on the Severn heading downstream from Shrewsbury. They may be under siege."

He sounded exasperated and weary.

I thought, *Has losing his mare made Father doubtful and depressed? I know for certain that he has been very unhappy about losing her. All the Normans love their horses. Sometimes Mother says he loves the mare more than her. I know it is not true, but it is not entirely false either.*

I wished I could see their faces as they talked, but knew I was lucky to even be hearing them.

"Peter," she now sounded awake, comforting and sad. "Even if King Henry has the Earl caught at Shrewsbury, what can we do but continue on? What if we were to give in this week and Belesme's army came over the hill next week? No, we have to hold out because this is the land of Earl Robert of Belesme before it is the land of King Henry. At least that's what you told me when the Earl left."

"Yes," he now sounded more confident. I wondered if she had said what he wanted her to say. He continued, "But if the Earl had surrendered will the King not bring him here to tell us to surrender also? Perhaps the note does lie."

I did not hear them talk again until Mother rose to help with breakfast. I lay there trying to devise my own plan to escape.

***

We drank water and ate a third of a thin slice of cold, fried horse meat for breakfast that morning. The slice was about as large as a slice of bacon. I felt almost as hungry, after eating, as I had before I sat down. I wondered if the lack of porridge meant that we were out of oats. Then I wondered what we were to feed the stallion and colt, for they always had some oats in addition to grass.

When Aethel and I brought the plates back to the kitchen, Mother and Mildred were talking about the day ahead. By the look on Mother's face, I could tell that she was not happy. Her lips were shut tight. I thought, *Is she still upset by what Father said this morning?*

"Yes," she said. "Loose meat sausage. And nothing else."

Mildred was not angry. She looked as if she wanted to calm Mother but was too tired to do so. She answered, "Could make a soup. Then, it might not taste so much like horse."

"But we have no barley or oats for bread and no vegetables," said Mother.

I could feel my stomach grumbling at the mention of food. I hoped they would decide quickly and stop talking.

"We might have four carrots ready to harvest and in a stew-"

"They will be barely tasted," Mother interrupted her. "Sausage will be more filling. We can dice and cook the carrots into that."

"Frying it up like that will take no time at all." Mildred was becoming testy, "Cooking should be some work. Otherwise why bother?"

"Fine, today we will not bother. We will have more of the day to enjoy. You and I will work in the kitchen today boiling tallow. Ulrica and Edwina, you will enjoy the sunshine with the girls." As Mother said this, she moved over to the dry sink and took over for Edwina who was starting to wash the breakfast plates.

Edwina was happy to be free of work and went to the hall to be with Rowena who was still lying on her mattress.

Ulrica took Aethel and me out of the kitchen and into the warm sunshine. "If Mildred was not head cook," she said, "Aedrica would not have let her stay in there either. Aedrica can do all that alone, and Lord knows Mildred needs to rest. She does not look at all well."

We nodded politely. Ulrica hustled off towards the stable, probably to see Manfred and check how Godwin was doing with the base of the Maple tree. I motioned to Aethel, and we followed her, hand-in-hand.

When we came around the corner of the kitchen, I could clearly see Godwin with a very sharp axe chopping at a huge chunk of the tree trunk. I wondered, *Did he sharpen it yesterday for this?* The sight of him working hard made me breathe faster. *Where is Wulfstan?*

"Aethel, I do not want to watch him being punished. And, I need time to think of a plan," I whispered.

She gave me a puzzled look, as we wandered over by the wild Cherry tree. We sat, watching a couple of lapwings. The male and female were looking for food for their young who had hatched the day before. I could see their little heads in the nest built in the ferns and grass behind the cherry tree. The male lapwing with his big, dark green feathery plume on his head looked very proud

245

of his young ones. The female with her muted dark blue coloring was flying all around the castle yard. I could find no reason for her to fly all over, but the mother bird did not answer me when I asked her why she did it.

Neither of us was in the mood to play tag or walk around the castle yard or go fishing in the imaginary pond in the pig pen, so I sat there on this warm, early summer day trying to think of a way to get out of the castle. I wondered, *Will Aethel get in trouble if she helps me escape the castle?*

Aethel spoke suddenly, "I worry about my grandmother. She is my only, my only…"

I thought, *Her only what? Her only parent? Her father died in battle last year. Her mother died years ago. Is she afraid Mildred will die?*

"She will be fine," I said.

I thought one of the clouds overhead looked like my father driving a wagon. *Will he be able to keep us all alive until the Earl arrives?*

I closed my eyes and imagined hearing the horn blowing from the Earl's army as it marched down the Oldbury road, or better yet the Shrewsbury road. I imagined I was helping to open the gates as Father and all the other men ran out to greet the Earl's troops.

But is this what will happen? I wondered. I did not

want to, but now my mind showed me a terrible scene. I imagined all of us lying in the castle yard, too tired to get up and open the gates for a herd of deer pounding their hooves on the gates, pounding to be let in.

I jumped. I could have sworn I heard pounding from the gates.

"Aethel, did you hear something?"

Aethel was looking up at the clouds. "No," she replied, "only the lapwings."

Father and Chrestian were on watch on the tower. They did not look like they had heard anyone pounding on the gates. Father stood stock still, watching for movement in the army camp.

"Aethel," I asked, "do you think my father will get us through this alive?"

She picked up a twig. "Does it matter what we think?" she asked.

"What do you mean?"

"We are children," she said. "We have the same chores and games and things to do whether we think this way or that."

"Oh," I said. I did not agree, but did not know how to argue against her point of view either.

"Can you think of any way to stop the siege?"

"No," she said in a small voice.

"Neither can I," I admitted. "Could one of us climb the tower to see what we need to do?"

"I am not willing to go up there, and you have tried over and over to get up there, and it never works. Why do you and Rowena keep trying to come up with plans?"

I hugged my knees up under my chin and did not answer. I thought, *She will never understand why Rowena and I want to see outside, how seeing what is going on makes all the difference. She never understands why I like going on errands to get to see people and know what they are doing.*

The sun was directly overhead; I decided to go see Rowena. Aethel agreed to come along. Rowena was resting on her mattress in the great hall. She was awake, so we sat down, cross-legged on her mattress.

"Where have you been?" Rowena asked.

"Out by the cherry tree," I said. "The sun is bright out there. Do you want to come out?"

"I want to, but I...maybe tomorrow."

"We should plan on that. Right, Aethel?"

Aethel nodded. Then she spoke up, "Grandmother is not feeling well today. Perhaps you will both be better tomorrow."

Rowena looked over to where Mildred's mattress

was at night. "The mattress is not there. So she is working, right? What is wrong with her?"

"She has a cough. I thinks she has not had enough food."

"We all need more food," I said. "Not only you and Mildred. Do you think the Earl's army will arrive today?"

Neither of them answered.

After Rowena fell asleep again, I crept to the pig shed to look at the ladder we had used to climb on the great hall roof. I tried lifting it and remembered why we had both carried it before. Despair hit me at the thought that I must do this without her.

I grabbed a coil of rope and examined it. The horn sounded twice, forcing me to put the rope back and go hide in the kitchen.

***

Mother was dishing spoonfuls of sausage onto plates, while Ulrica and Edwina were putting the plates on trays. Mildred was sitting on a stool by the cooking fire. Sitting while others bustled was so unlike her that Aethel asked her if she was well.

Mildred could hardly reply for coughing and clearing her throat. "I - hahem - will be fine. Hahem.

Needed - hahem - to rest a bit." Mildred motioned for Aethel to go help with the plates.

Mildred slowly trailed out of the kitchen carrying only her own plate.

I sat beside Rowena on her mattress and helped her eat the sausage. As she ate I told her about my visit to the pig shed. Rowena did her best to eat as much as she could, but she only could eat about two-thirds. I finished her portion.

She informed me that the wall behind the stable wall had no hook or point to catch a rope end.

"Yes," I said. "I saw that. But can we use the rope somewhere else or some other way?"

"Only on the tower, and I do not want…"

I wiped a tear from her cheek, and she smiled weakly.

Father stood and motioned for everyone's attention. "Men," he said, "help clear away the tables and lay out the mattresses for the night. We should not have entertainment on a night before the Sabbath. We should go to rest...as we are all tired from a day of work."

I was confused. I had not worked, nor had most of the others. From what I had seen, the only workers had been Godwin and Wulfstan at chopping, Mother in the kitchen, and Sir Jehann and William who were now on the tower.

Everyone was glancing at Rowena and then looking away. Then I noticed they were all looking the same way at Mildred and whispering.

I decided to try to climb the tower this night with the rope. The nearly full moon would be fine for showing me the way. Perhaps the man on watch would go to the privies or run some errand and I could creep up there. When the women went to the dressing room, I excused myself to go to the privies. Unfortunately, Aethel said she wanted to go with me. I groaned. *Why*, I thought, *is she ruining my plan? I will have to get on the tower tomorrow. Perhaps I can talk sweetly to my father after mass.*

DAY 32, WHITSUNDAY

"Grandmother!" Aethel cried out.

Her cry woke us all. I slept only a few feet from them and propped myself up on my mattress to see what the matter was. My mother, Ulrica and Bert came over to Mildred's mattress.

"Mildred has a bad fever of the lungs," said Ulrica. "She should rest today."

Everyone was silent. I chewed on my upper lip. I wondered, *Will Mildred die? That is unthinkable.*

I folded my blanket and went over to hold Aethel's hand. I reached for her, but she was busy tucking blankets around Mildred.

Ulrica told Mother to go get some cool, wet cloths for her forehead. Mother left for the cistern, and soon after Ulrica said she was going to the kitchen to get some herbs and warm water for a healing tea.

Godwin went to fetch the priest who had already gone to the little altar to prepare for Sabbath mass. Father Cuthbert came to the great hall and said a few Latin prayers over her to return to health. He declared that mass would be said with her health as the chief prayer of intention.

Ulrica returned and, looking at Father, told

everyone, "I am out of black elder flower, the herb I need for Mildred's tea. I have a mustard poultice for her chest, but must have the tea to cure her. The tree blooms in May and I have not been able to go out to harvest the flowers I will need for this year."

Tears were running down Aethel's face. Her eyes were now red and her cheeks were really wet as if she was swimming in the stream. I could not help but cry too.

Through my own tears, I looked over at Rowena lying on her mat by the window. I thought, *Oh, will she die too? She is as weak as Mildred yesterday. But Rowena is getting food, being made to eat all the food brought up to her. Maybe she will stay healthy.*

***

Even Father Cuthbert looked thin in his robes as he said the mass at the gray stone altar. He had always been flabby fleshed, but not really fat. Now he was thin. I wondered, *Is he the hand of God?* He read from the book and made prayers for Mildred. *Is God still looking out for us if the hand is withering too?*

Aethel was kneeling in the front row, on the other side of Mother. Aethel was sobbing so much that she could not possibly be saying the Latin phrases with the rest of us. Bert, right in front of me, was holding the book open for

Father Cuthbert. with his jaw clenched tight.

Father, standing to my right, had a stony, sad expression. I felt sad, but without the stony. My mother looked more angry than sad. My mother put her left arm over Aethel's shoulder, but it did not calm either one of them. Aethel kept on sobbing, and my mother's hand started clenching. I started feeling fear, but not of Mildred dying. I thought, *Mother's temper is steaming now, and Aethel's sobs are providing the heat. When her anger reaches the boiling point probably right after the mass, it will be a bad idea to be anywhere nearby. Can I calm her down some way?*

As soon as Father Cuthbert said the Pax Vobiscum, I went around to Aethel and knelt beside her, partly to comfort Aethel and partly to get her away from Mother's temper.

"Cheer up," I said. "Ulrica will find some herbs in that big cabinet. Will she not, Mother?"

I smiled weakly up at Mother who did not smile back. She simply walked away from the altar without me. But Father, beside her now, could see the upcoming storm. Sir Jehann walked over to them. I thought, *Did he also see that Mother was about to unleash a fury?*

"Aethel, what are you doing?" I asked.

She looked at me like I was simple. "Crying," she

said.

"Yes," I said. "I see that. Look at how angry your crying has made my mother."

"Good," she said.

Bert put his arm around Aethel. Her sobbing worsened.

I thought, *What does she mean good? Is she crying on purpose? Is it some plan?*

Aethel did not stop and looked like she could hardly breathe. Bert grabbed her and tried to lead her back to the hall. He muttered that he would take her to see their grandmother.

The anger storm broke behind us as we reached the hall. Bert looked at me and nodded. I started walking slowly over towards my parents as if drawn to them.

"Peter!" Mother yelled, "It does not have to happen!"

"You have said that a couple of times now and you are still wrong!" He now looked as angry as her.

He continued after a pause to catch his breath, "It does have to! We have to wait for the Earl! We cannot open the gates to gather a few herbs!"

Please Mother, I thought, *see that he is right. Please let me have a chance to explain how I could go over the wall. Please.*

Edwina, who was standing right behind Mother, broke in, "Oh, surely you do not still believe the Earl is going to come and save us?"

Godwin pulled Edwina to his side and put a finger to his lips. He was trying to remind her that it was not her place to talk. I wondered if he was avoiding Father's anger or waiting his turn to speak.

"He has given up on us," Mother shouted, "or he is captured like the King's messengers say! Are we all to die before he gets here?" Her question and her attention were solely for Father.

I thought, *Why will she not go take a walk to calm down? Can she not see she is talking about surrender? Maybe I need to get her attention to whisper to her. She could ruin everything.*

I took a step closer to Father, as my stomach tightened further.

"Oh, Aedrica, calm down," he said, "It does not matter if we give up on the Earl, our rightful lord, now or later, or earlier. Disloyalty is still disloyalty. We have sworn to stand by him whether King Henry likes him or not, whether we like him or not. Can you open the gates to the King's men today knowing that the Earl may arrive tomorrow with a siege-raising army looking for his people? Is that not what you told me?"

Father Cuthbert cleared his throat. "Aedrica, obey your husband," he said.

I was the only one who even glanced at him.

Of course no one was listening to Father Cuthbert, for his advice was useless. But I wondered whether I could say anything that might dispel the anger storm better than him.

Mother looked at Father for a few moments. Everyone knew that she had started this fight and it was her turn to answer.

"All along I have listened patiently to you and done my wifely duty, holding your position. Even defending your position to the other women. But Mildred can only be saved by one of us going outside. If not, the rest of us will follow her soon. If the Earl cared, he would not be letting us grow sickly for lack of food."

"Oh yes," she continued, "he would have come by now or sent rations or more men-at-arms. An oath goes two ways, Peter. He must care for us. He does not, so we are not the ones breaking the oath. There is no loss of your precious Norman honor."

As Mother said all this, the people around me shuffled on their feet uncertainly. I realized they were the ones affected by oath giving and breaking. The men were the ones who had to face Earl Robert's wrath, if he came back. The men-at-arms and Saxons who lived here also had face the army's stones, arrows and swords. They feared the army outside. They wanted to know if starvation was better than what the King's soldiers would do to them.

I could see Father's reaction was quite different. He was exasperated. I thought, *Now is the time for him to save us. I am sure of that.*

I opened my mouth to say something, but he started speaking first.

"Aedrica, my dear, you do not understand. The Earl is our liege. No matter how he treats us, we obey and serve." He moved closer to her.

Sir Jehann looked like he wanted to speak but Edwina interrupted, "The King is Earl Robert's liege! Was not the Earl unfaithful to him?"

Father continued looking at Mother and spoke as if to her alone, as if he had not heard Edwina standing only two feet away, "We must be faithful, it is our duty. Without this duty, what are we?"

I thought he did not expect anyone to answer. He certainly looked, with a smile in his eyes, like he had proven himself right.

But my father was wrong.

Jehann now walked right up to him and spoke forcefully, "We must look to the way the world is here today, Peter." He paused for effect and I wondered if this was to be one of Sir Jehann's long speeches.

"We have been faithful, very full of faith. We have held this castle as we were told. But we do not have the food to remain in this siege. If this sick old woman dies and we give this old woman a Saxon burial, we will only have a couple of days of firewood. The other women are all starving too. That girl who sleeps all day in the hall is not much better than the old woman. Of course, we are not here to protect them."

I thought, *What? Not here to protect us?*

Godwin's hands clenched, and I could hear his teeth grinding. I realized my fists were clenched too.

Jehann did not see Godwin and kept on talking. "The Earl has charged us with protecting these buildings, his castle. But still we must think of the servants somewhat. As to food…You know we have almost none left. Certainly not enough to feed men for strength before a battle if the Earl returns. For we need the good, strong meal to make the good, strong fight. If we must surrender now, where is the loss of honor? Can the Earl ask more of us than this?"

"There is no oath breaking here and so no dishonor," he continued. "We must simply admit defeat. I am a proud Norman. I will speak with Lord Roger de

Montgomery this morning. He will most likely ask for my head and I will give it with strength and courage, as befits my Norman blood. I will go saddle my stallion now. Peter, if you wish to ride out with me, you may do so."

Manfred roused and went to the stable for it was his job to saddle the stallion.

Mother had no anger left in her face. Father also had no steel left in his spine. They embraced. Then Father beckoned that I should come to him.

"I will go with Jehann. We will make a peace that will leave you and the other Saxons alive. Most likely, I will live also after I make pledges to the King. If I do not, Aedrica, go to your brother in Quatford. He will care for you. Most likely I will see you this evening," he said.

I tried to speak. I wanted to tell him not to go, but I could not. All that came out was a sob. He looked at me and kissed my forehead. I wondered whether this would be the last time I would see him. Then he went to the hall to fetch his armor and a cloth for a truce flag. Sir Jehann followed to the great hall.

Mother told all the women and girls to go into the kitchen. I did not go in, but stood by the door of the kitchen. She gave me a stern look and told me to stay there. I did not know what to do. I thought, *Should I go help open the gates? Should I go with the men? Should I*

go try to get a view of it all from the tower? I wanted to
stop it all and save Father.

Mother came over to me and tried to comfort me with an arm over my shoulder. I was not in the mood for a hug.

"What is your question, Maud?"

"I feel so useless that Father is going. What can I do? I wanted to be the one to help save us, but your anger has done that," I confessed.

Father Cuthbert asked Manfred what to do. Manfred told him to keep praying. Manfred motioned to Godwin and they headed for the kitchen.

Mother wiped a tear from her face and kissed my forehead.

"I was not trying to change Peter's strategy. I simply want us all to survive. That fever will spread from Mildred to the others if we do not get the medicine. And you, my dear, have done much. Do not ever doubt that."

I moved aside for Godwin and Manfred as Ulrica met them at the kitchen door and handed them a large, leather drawstring pouch for the black elder flowers.

"Now mind you," she said. "it must be the flowers - not the leaves - of the black elder. They are white flowers. The closest stand of them is across the river." She pointed out to the northeast. "The trees are about fifty feet on the other side of the river. Over there, you know by the river crossing and then fifty feet that way. Now, you know which trees I mean. Oh, and if the flowers have already bloomed and dropped as is most likely, then pick them up off the ground. For nothing else that grows within a day's walk will do."

Manfred kissed her on the forehead and assured her he would find it and return.

Bert and Wulfstan were a few feet away in the castle yard. Wulfstan motioned and went up the tower. He blew the horn several times so that the King's army would pay attention to what was about to happen.

Bert met Godwin and Manfred at the gates and the three of them started to lift the bar on the left gate. The wooden gate with large iron hinges proved hard to open, having been shut for so many days. I wondered, *Will the army rush in and attack us? Will Wulfstan have the battle he prefers?*

I was wrong to worry. No one rushed in.

Chrestian and William were at the open gates with their sword waiting for Sir Jehann and my father. While the brothers stood there, Chrestian whispered something to William and then limped over to where Edwina was standing on the other side of the kitchen door. Before Edwina could react, Chrestian kissed her on the right cheek.

Edwina stood there speechless.

Mother muttered that with any luck Godwin had not seen that.

The stallion carrying Sir Jehann trotted over to Chrestian. Sir Jehann gave him a helping hand up. Then they and my father trotted through the gates, William jogging behind them down the hill.

We all stood there by the kitchen door, quite still until the four men were out of sight down the path. Then Mother shook herself slightly as if waking up from a daydream. She faced Edwina.

"We had better cook some breakfast," she said with authority in her voice. "We have not eaten yet and it is late morning."

Edwina, still caressing her cheek, asked what we should eat.

Mother headed off to the vegetable garden to see what could be picked.

Ulrica led me into the kitchen. She handed me a large clay bowl full of water. She said, "Go help keep Mildred's fever down. Here is more water for the washcloth to mop her face and arms. Stay there with her until I call you. Call me if she gets worse. I will be needed here."

She bent over the cooking fire. The wood embers from last night were still lying there and the fire was completely out. Seeing the embers made me realize how hungry I was. As Ulrica started to clean the ashes, I walked slowly, trying not to spill the water. I thought, *Is this the best I can do to help all this?*

When I stepped inside, it took my eyes a minute to adjust to the dark. No one had moved the tables or lit candles in here this morning before mass.

As soon as my eyes adjusted, I took the bowl over to where Mildred was sleeping with a thin woolen blanket over her. Aethel was wiping her face with a nearly dry washcloth.

"Aethel is better," said Rowena." We can help Mildred and we know that Father and Uncle Manfred have gone to get the fever herb, Here, sit down."

"Thank you," I said. "Did you see my parents fight?"

"I heard it from the doorway."

"I do not know what to do," I said. "Father, Jehann, Chrestian and William went over to the army camp. They may not return for a long while. I do not know. Godwin and Manfred went off for the herb. They are not returned either. Wulfstan and Bert are on watch. Father Cuthbert is praying at the altar. Oh, and Chrestian kissed Edwina."

Rowena exploded with curiosity, "Really? On the lips?"

"On the cheek. Your father did not see it."

She hugged her knees to her chest as if to keep her excitement in. "No, but he will know. He has a way of knowing."

"Rowena, do you think he likes her? Could any man like her?"

Her face showed her doubt. "Mother used to say that you never can know what men will like."

"Maybe," I said. "But does this particular man like Edwina?"

"Father will find out from him and his brother William. What was the look on her face?" Rowena's own face was now all attention.

"She was startled and then she was all smiling and tender. She kept caressing her cheek. It was thoroughly sickening," I said.

Rowena giggled and I giggled too. Even Aethel smiled.

Then we heard Wulfstan yell something. I ran to the door, and Rowena followed me. Rowena clung to the doorway for support.

Wulfstan was pointing to the gate.

William and Chrestian came running in. Rowena stayed in the doorway, while I went running with the women and Bert to the gates to meet them. Mother was carrying two mugs of ale for them.

"Mother, is it over now? The waiting, is it over? And why is Father not with them?" I whispered in her left ear.

Mother put an arm around my shoulders fondly. "Yes, no, and now we wait to hear William tell us what the terms are and where your father is. Then we will wait for something else. That is how time passes."

Once William had caught his breath and drunk his ale, he began to speak.

"We go and the knight William de Montgomery is speaking to us when we enter the camp. He is saying that his older brother Lord Roger de Montgomery is back at his lands east of here. They accept our surrender and will send their squires - here to watch over us in our tower."

He took another sip. "They send a messenger to Lord Roger de Montgomery. Jehann and Peter are to stay there in the camp until Lord Roger returns. That is maybe tomorrow, maybe the day after."

We all stood quietly a moment, taking in what he had said. I realized, *Mother is right, the siege is not over in a second. Life at Bridgnorth Castle will take days to get back to...well, not normal, but back to not starving and not confined.*

"Are we allowed to come and go? Can we go hunt or fish? Will they feed Father and Jehann? Will they be given ale?" I asked.

"Yes," he replied, "we may leave but the squires and knights who watch the castle from all sides may not have been told. We must have - we must be careful."

Chrestian nodded and continued the explanation, "They are within the tent of Sir William himself. Their hands lay bound but they will be given food and drink, perhaps wine even. They will be treated with hospitality - as Normans."

Mother smiled at me and said softly, "They will live, my dear. They are being treated well."

Mother asked Chrestian and William to go light candles in the hall. They would be brought some soup. Ulrica, Edwina and I carried pitchers of ale and bowls of onion soup to the hall. Mother carried some soup to the tower for Wulfstan, while the rest of us ate in the hall.

When we were half done eating, Wulfstan called out that Manfred and Godwin were back. Ulrica went running to them. They had the black elder flowers in the pouch on Manfred's belt. They were carrying their hoods in their hands strangely, like they were trying to keep large, wet rocks in the curve of the hood. Manfred explained to Ulrica that the hoods held several river eels that they had "found" under their feet as they crossed the river.

I chuckled at his obvious lie.

Manfred also reported seeing a number of men on horseback riding up the path.

Ulrica asked them if they had seen any men watching the castle. Godwin said yes there had been one Norman squire but they sneaked around him easily.

Ulrica took them to the kitchen so she could boil the medicine tea for Mildred and feed them soup.

Mother told Edwina and me to go bring more pitchers of ale from the cellar for the squires coming to watch over us.

"May I go up on the tower first, Mother?" I said. "I will fetch the ale, but first I want to see. You went up there with Wulfstan's soup so it must be safe."

Her eyebrows pinched closer together. "You will not relent, will you? Hmm."

She walked me over to the base of the tower and called out to Wulfstan.

His long, gray mustache appeared over the railing above. "Yes, she may come up. The word has gone out to the squires around us, I think."

"You may go up for a fast look. Then you go fetch that ale as I told you."

She headed back to the kitchen. I glanced at the hall. Rowena was leaning against the doorway. I grinned and waved furiously for her to come.

She started wandering towards the tower, going around the garden altogether. I wondered, *Should I go help her? Does she want to go up? Has she changed her mind about being scared of going up?*

"Rowena, do you want to go up on the tower? Mother and Wulfstan say it is safe enough. Our fathers have been safe enough up here."

She nodded. "I do want to see the army. I hate this tower and am rather scared, but you are going with me, right?"

I nodded back. I was fearful, not only of being hurt on the tower. I was fearful for what Lord Roger de Montgomery would do to my father. I was fearful for what the army might do to us. I took a deep breath. Now I would be able to see it all and conquer the fear.

Rowena was now in the base of the tower with me.

"You go first, Maud. You deserve it for getting your mother to agree, right?"

I shook my head. "You go first. I will be here behind you, so you cannot fall."

She grabbed a rung and started climbing. Then I heard Edwina come up behind me. "Hurry up! I want to go up there too."

HISTORICAL NOTE

The old saying that Rome wasn't built in a day is true of castles as well. Bridgnorth started as a small Saxon fort with several wooden buildings and some sort of wooden fortification.

In 1101, Earl Robert of Belesme supported Robert of Normandy in an attempt for the English throne against his brother King Henry I. Henry retained the throne and announced that Earl Robert would be stripped of his land and castles. Earl Robert decided to move his chapel and operations from Quatford (which is no longer on the map) to Bridgnorth, presumably for its defensible position. He built a high wall around the existing Saxon fort and a church beside the castle.

In 1102, all of Earl Robert's castles were besieged by King Henry's army. Robert of Belesme was captured at Shrewsbury. However, in 1104 he reconciled to the King and was given his former lands again.

This is basically all the history books have to say about the sieges. The lives and fate of the people in the three castles are not written in the chronicles of that day.

Strangely, Bridgnorth castle was besieged at least three times, twice by the King's army. In a later siege, the hill beside the castle was leveled off to fit a large siege engine. The hill then somehow got the name Pam Pudding

Hill. Before that siege a second wall was also built around the trading town which grew to the north of Bridgnorth Castle.

No mention is made in the chronicles of that day that a siege engine was used in the siege of 1102, but given the Norman siege tactics of the time some sort of siege weaponry would have been used.

LIST OF SUGGESTED BOOKS

The Smashing Saxons. Horrible Histories Collection. Terry Deary. Scholastic, 2006.

Growing Up With The Norman Conquest. Alfred Duggan and C. Walter Hodges. Pantheon Books, 1966.

Wales. Anna Hestler. New York: Marshall Cavendish Corp., 2001.

The Middle Ages. Sarah Howarth. Viking, 1993.

The Games Treasury. Merilyn Mohr. New York: Houghton Mifflin, 1997.

The Normans. Anne & Barry Steel. Illustrated by Barry Wood. Hove, UK: Wayland Publishing Ltd., 1987.

Castles. Beth Smith. London: Watts LB, 1988.

Saxon, Viking and Norman (Men at Arms Series 85). Terence Wise and Gerry Embleton. London: Osprey Publishing, 1979.

Visit Castle Bridgnorth and all these characters at
www.preciousnormanhonor.wordpress.com.